THE FAÇADES

THE FACADES

A NOVEL

ERIC LUNDGREN

OVERLOOK DUCKWORTH

NEW YORK • LONDON

This edition first published in hardcover in the United States and the United Kingdom in 2013 by Overlook Duckworth, Peter Mayer Publishers, Inc.

NEW YORK
141 Wooster Street
New York, NY 10012
www.overlookpress.com
For bulk and special sales, please contact sales@overlookny.com,
or write us at above address.

LONDON
30 Calvin Street
London E1 6NW
info@duckworth-publishers.co.uk
www.ducknet.co.uk
For bulk and special sales, please contact sales@duckworth-publishers.co.uk,
or write us at the above address.

ISBN 978-1-4683-0687-3 US
ISBN 978-0-7156-4767-7 UK
FIRST EDITION
1 3 5 7 9 10 8 6 4 2

For Eleanor
who walks with me through cities

We believe, so to speak, that this great building exists, and then we see, now here, now there, one or another small corner of it.

—WITTGENSTEIN, *On Certainty*

"You can resume your flight whenever you like," they said to me, "but you will arrive at another Trude, absolutely the same, detail by detail. The world is covered by a sole Trude, which does not begin and does not end. Only the name of the airport changes."

—CALVINO, *Invisible Cities*

THE FACADES

1

I USED TO DRIVE DOWNTOWN EVERY NIGHT, LOOKING FOR MY wife. The rush hour traffic was across the median and I traveled the westbound lane of I-99 without delay or impediment, sure I was going the wrong way. The city assembled itself, scattered lights in the old skyscrapers meandering the night sky like notes on a staff. What could I have hoped to find there? People didn't just disappear, I thought at the time. They left fingerprints, notes, receipts, echoes. If Molly had walked from her opera rehearsal to the corner deli and had not materialized there or returned, she must have left a residue behind. I expressed this view to the authorities after filing the missing person report at Trude's tenth precinct station. "It's not always a Hansel and Gretel type situation, you know," said the detective, a fellow named McCready who was apparently on the late shift alone, surrounded by dim idling computers. Crew-cutted and monobrowed, he looked like a man who repaired machinery with his bare hands. He listened to my story and took notes in his pocket pad, a mere scribe. On his desk, instead of a family picture, was a grainy photograph of

Wittgenstein. The matte frame was inscribed with a misquotation: THE CASE IS EVERYTHING THAT IS THE WORLD. McCready promised to call if anything turned up, but I was in no mood to wait. I set out on my own through the streets, my pockets jammed with plastic evidence bags. I was a student of sidewalks. Tracing Molly's possible steps in widening circles, I returned each night to the Opera House empty-handed, the watchman nodding me in.

This night watchman had been the last to see Molly and became a de facto authority on her disappearance, even though he was "not that perceptive," as he admitted later in interviews. He seemed hardly to notice me as I went in and out. His good eye browsed in my direction, then slumped back into the couch of his cheek.

She was projected outward from my mind, a wavering image across the city. I began the nights as a stalker, then faded to a stumbler, a somnambulist. I rounded every corner with the conviction that she was near, but what I found in those deceptive and winding streets was only a series of dispersed apparitions. The curve of her spine in the shadow of a lamppost. The pattern of her freckles in a smattering of plaster dust. In the winking of a broken traffic signal, the green of her eyes.

You may not have come across our city, which they used to call halfway to everywhere, which is to say nowhere—stranded in the long and level void between the two coasts. As a lifelong resident, I will tell you right away: it is easy to get lost. "Lose yourself in Trude" was the tourist board slogan for a while, but it never caught on. It was too apt. Visitors, attempting to describe their stay in Trude, often resorted to the German term *platzangst*. The city fathers should be blamed for this common feeling, this anxiety that one is trying, but failing, to cross a vast and endless square. Using Sitte's *City Planning According to Artistic Principles* as their guide, our patriarchs designed a downtown that still looks beautiful on a map, hailed as "the Munich of the Midwest" throughout the late 1890s. The twentieth century was unkind. Grand hotels, windowed with cardboard, still advertised ten-dollar rooms on their outer walls. Decrepit mansions hung on the boulevards, spattered with graffiti. Money, with its gaseous tendencies to rise and escape, drifted to the suburbs of Sherwood Forest and New Arcadia.

I was a prematurely old man wandering the grid, such as it was. Sitte proscribed the 90-degree intersection, so I navigated narrow side lanes and cul-de-sacs. These byways abruptly ended in small plazas with ivy-choked fountains and statues eroded by rain and snow. The statues stood, per Sitte's instruction, in the corners rather than the centers (he determined this by watching where children placed snowmen in their yards). Alleys snaked between buildings, dark arteries of criminal life. If one were to believe the hysterical editorialists of the *Trude Trumpet*, lawbreakers infested the city, lurking behind fire escapes and monuments to civic progress. They slept in abandoned buildings under ghost signs for knickerbockers, cobblers, and grain.

These were the streets I walked that May, after Molly left to buy an egg for her throat and did not return. It was an unusually cool month, but this was lost on me. The rain felt wet only. Each night I began at the Opera House, near the corner of Hamsun Avenue and Sinuous Lane, and continued past the sturdy pillars of the Central Library, down the secluded alleys with their old clock shops. Watchmakers squinted at me through their loupes. I occasionally found a sodden poster for one of the

5

operas my wife had performed in. The posters carried raves from the *Trumpet* ("Molly Norberg is no fat lady . . . stunning!"). They were gashed and faded, and her face was almost made up beyond recognition, but I was already losing the tender image in my memory, so I peeled them from walls and lampposts and stashed them in the trunk of her car.

MOLLY'S VOICE COACH, old Frau Huber, and her whiskery husband lived on the otherwise uninhabited second floor of the Ambassador Hotel. They owned two flats across from each other at the end of the hall and left the doors open, except on the increasingly rare occasions when they gave lessons. The two apartments could barely contain their mountains of sheet music and LPs. Their twin pianos and string instruments stood in progressive stages of disassembly. When I arrived at the Ambassador, the Hubers were playing Beethoven's Sonata for Four Hands on opposite sides of the hall. It seemed too soon for music. The sonata was discordant. The piano tuner had not been around in a while. Mice clambered from the Ambassador's cracked drywall and fat feral cats waddled the halls. I had to shake the rusted room service bell to get Frau Huber's attention. She raised her knobby, arthritic hands from the keyboard as if I'd caught her at something. Her husband's chords continued minus a melody. She reached back and clapped her trembling hand over mine.

"My poor boy," she whispered. "You must be hungry."

She went to the kitchen to make tea, while Herr Huber entered cracking his knuckles and joined me at a table piled with books and scores, where we could barely see each other. A tin of stale chocolates was produced. Frau Huber had been a maternal figure for Molly, whose own parents had died young, and as I accepted an ancient truffle, it occurred to me that I thought of Frau Huber as Molly's mother, my mother-in-law. Huber had Molly's nose. Her white hair was neatly worked into a circular braid around the back of her skull. She was prone, as Molly was, to walk to the refrigerator, crack open an egg on the counter, and with one swift motion, deposit the yoke down her throat while crushing the shell in her hand. She was a mezzo, like Molly. My wife had probably spent more time with Frau Huber than she had at home in the months preceding her disappearance. Looking at the old woman just then, as steam wheezed from the kettle, was like looking at the future Molly I'd always thought I would see. Her husband sat snug in his vest across the table, still tapping out the Beethoven on the stained oak. As his English was limited and mine was impaired, we didn't make much of a conversational duo.

"There are things music can say that words can't," Frau Huber said, dropping sugar cube after sugar cube into her tea. The morning *Trumpet* was awkwardly placed in the center of the table, its thick inky headline unavoidable: DIVA VANISHES DOWNTOWN. "There are also things music can't say," she added.

"Did you notice anything strange about Molly at her last lesson?" I asked.

"Nothing strange," she said. "You talk like a policeman."

"They come *twice* already!" Herr Huber barked.

"Interrogation makes him nervous," Frau Huber said, pushing the old cookie tin at me. It was etched with a scene of two children, hand in hand, following a narrow path through a dark forest.

* * *

THERE WAS AN old cathedral downtown, a cloister of tradition-alists who had run afoul of the local archbishop. Mass had been read in Latin there until the diocese disowned the building and its small congregation. I went in when the weather was bad. It was a dry place to wait it out, though the roof leaked, and a long water stain marred the ceiling mosaic, which depicted the saints and missionaries who had brought the faith to Trude. Gold cherubs and silver doves kept watch over the looted altar. Stained glass windows, broken by tossed rocks, lay in disarray on the floor, like a jigsaw puzzle abandoned by a distracted child. The fragments half spelled out a holy face, a fractured sky. These, too, reminded me of Molly; I collected the stained glass shards in my blazer pockets so that I might later assemble them into a coherent image. I'd once sat in this cathedral and listened to her sing the Brahms Alto Rhapsody under those windows.

I always assumed I was alone there, waiting out the rain. One night, however, a flashlight beam pierced the darkness from high above. It seemed to issue from the organ pipes. A priest, unshaven, in a rumpled cassock pocked with pipe burns, paced along the massive gray cylinders, looking small. "Can I help you find anything?" cried the distant, annoyed voice.

"My name is Norberg," I said. "I'm looking for my wife."

A younger man with long blond hair and a tuxedo shirt emerged in front of the organ pipes. "Your what?" he asked.

I held up an opera poster—one of the more realistic ones, in which my wife's face could be discerned behind the cosmetics. The priest shined his flashlight over Molly's pale and freckled cheeks, her snub nose. I'd once started counting her freckles with pedantic slowness, one by one, until she'd pushed me away in a blizzard of white teeth and red curls.

"Oh my," he said, peering down. "*She* was *your* wife?"

"Is. Is my wife."

"She sang for us once," said the younger man. "I was the music minister then."

"I know. I was in the pews listening."

"Mr. Norbert," the priest called, apparently deafened by standing too close to organ pipes, "did you see the brick rustlers outside?"

"Stop being paranoid," the music minister snapped.

I shuffled the glass in my blazer pockets. "No." Only a few feet from me, a stone angel wing fell from far above and smashed to grit on the back of a pew.

"These bricks are very valuable on the black market," the priest said. "You didn't see anyone?"

"I saw some guys out there," I said. "I think they were just cooling their heels."

"Better not think about it," the music minister said. "Your wife came here very often before she . . . before the . . . did you know that?"

"No."

The music minister's face was hairless, and I wondered if he shaved with stained glass. "Yes, she used to come in at night, much like you do now."

"I like the building," I said.

"She seemed . . . did you notice this, Father? She seemed to take a special interest in our eunuchs."

"Your eunuchs?"

"I think they're well done, don't you?" The music minister

took the priest's flashlight and shined it on the chubby, sexless figures chiseled in high relief above a transept arch. They floated in the rafters, lips parted, delighting in their buoyant, chubby flesh. "Of course, so many things are well done in this cathedral, it's almost impossible to know where to look. The problem of the baroque. Since the diocese abandoned us, we try to look at the bright side. Perhaps if the cathedral loses some of its beauties, like the windows and the mosaic, visitors in the future will not find it so . . . so *excessive*."

"Why do they want *our* bricks?" asked the priest. "Aren't there enough vacant brick buildings around here? Do they want them to be blessed?"

"And that *voice*." The music minister spread his arms, as if to embrace the organ pipes, as if only such an improbable embrace could capture the power and range of Molly's singing. "My God, what a voice she had."

MY FINAL ENCOUNTER was the kind that keeps most people away from downtown Trude at night. I was walking back to the car, parked in the plaza at Sinuous Lane and Dead Mayor Boulevard. I had stopped to examine an evocative piece of vandalism. Some part time provocateur, some nocturnal sower of unease and distress, had upended the golden triangle of a pedestrian crossing sign. The stick figure, so resolute in his forward stride, his whole body arched toward its destination, now was a man in free fall, his limbs four useless black slabs. I admired the vandal's work until I felt the point of a knife graze my spine. The knifepoint was soon followed by a weirdly calming hand on my shoulder, to hold me in place, and I was momentarily uncertain whether to tense up or relax. It had been a while since I'd been touched. "I'm going to take your wallet," said the high tenor voice behind me. "Okay, great!" I replied, ruefully recalling the sum of cash my employer had given me to "tide me over" for the weekend. The lump was removed. I listened to the thug count bills with the swift, satisfied stroke of a pulp novelist turning manuscript pages. He had lowered the knife, so I turned to face him. His scrawniness was mitigated by a puffy white down coat. His cheeks looked like cutting boards, scuffed and hard. After pocketing the cash he evaluated me. "Christ, what happened to you, man?" he asked. I did not reply. He flipped the wallet in my direction. "Thank you!" I said. I did not tell my assailant that he reminded me of my son, who suffered from a skin condition, and who had been home alone each and every night of my search. Every night I wandered, pursuing my private and degraded film of Molly through the streets, Kyle had been completely alone.

I lingered in that plaza long after the marshmallow of the thug's coat had dissolved into the alley's dark. My only company was the bronze statue of Mayor Trudenhauser, after whom our city had been named. As the story went, he'd truncated the name of our town from Trudenhauser to Trude following a series of public and private failures in the late 1890s that left him listless and afraid. He cast a plump shadow on the cobblestones. Smoking my last cigarette, I realized that these nighttime expeditions had to end, that I was not going to find anything here, that I had to start driving home instead of downtown after work. Beside me, the bronze mayor contemplated the unmoving hands of his giant pocket watch. His heavy eyes, flecked with rust and rain, looked almost human.

2

OUR HOUSE DATED FROM 1909 AND STOOD AT A SLANT; IT WAS rife with charming defects. My son's favorite pastime, as a child, had been to roll marbles from one end of the living room to the other. The marbles rumbled quickly across our uneven floorboards, and when they smacked the front door, leaping almost to the mail slot, Kyle beat his little hands together with delight. It was my job to confiscate his marbles when the game disturbed his mother's vocal exercises. He could make me feel criminal, regarding me tragically as I locked the marbles in a drawer just out of his reach. Now Kyle was sixteen. Molly had taken to calling him "the troubled teen we're harboring" with a cagey laugh. Her disappearance was just one in a long series of outrages against him, it seemed. He kept to his basement bedroom, tapping the keys of the computer that soaked him in a blue glow, while upstairs the keys of the grand piano turned gray with dust.

Molly hung over our crooked house like an absentee landlord. Commuting from couch to refrigerator to bed, I passed the grandfather clock an elderly admirer had given her, the mask she'd worn the first time she was in *Aida*, and other humbler manifestations—the notes she'd made herself and stuck to the fridge and the bulletin board: *buy paper towels*, *Sven to ophthalmologist*, and others whose meaning had become cryptic. It was heartbreaking to see her elegant cursive give way to my stiff carpenter's hand. I delayed buying paper towels and scheduling the eye appointment so that she would remain there, still pertinent to our lives. When I finally broke down and bought paper towels, I saved her Post-it in one of the plastic evidence bags, even as I asked myself what exactly it was evidence of. That she had once been here, doing very banal things like writing grocery lists? I was equally adamant about the piano practice chart taped to the refrigerator. Kyle had not practiced in months, so the chart that had once been filled with dutiful *X*s was now a blank grid. A few weeks after the last date had passed, I peeled it off the fridge—the tape was reluctant to give—and handed it to my son who was drying his hands at the sink. He crumpled it up and threw it away.

"What?" he said, catching my stare. "It's not like it's some kind of *holy relic*."

The cat-mauled armchair was about the only place I felt calm. The chair was the house's main remnant of our early relationship, our "spaghetti days" as Molly called them, back when she played roles such as Attendant #2 and Chorus Girl with Braids and intoned the occasional commercial jingle for money. The old tan chair was large and sturdy enough to support us both if she climbed over the side and onto my lap, as she often had in the spaghetti days. We bought the chair used and it survived our squalid apartments. Tolerated for sentimental reasons, it went into hiding when company came. I had always preferred it to the nicer seating Molly bought later, but now my love for it was exclusive (my son avoided the living room). I stationed it across from my new friend, the TV, and it was here, after drifting to sleep one evening, that I woke to encounter her again, near me, mere *feet* from me, singing Marthe in Gounod's *Faust* on our local public television station. "Molly? Molly?" I cried out, as I had in the dream I'd just woken from, but she continued singing, in French, of unrelated matters.

On the stairwell that night, I passed the three paintings of my wife. They were unsigned, having appeared in plain brown paper on our front step a few years back. The anonymous painter worked in the eroticized, hyperprecise style of Balthus. Molly's hair was a lurid blaze running through the series. The first painting hung at the foot of the staircase and showed Molly onstage in a crumbling amphitheater, wearing a toga, her body sturdier than the broken columns surrounding her. Hundreds of identical men with gray faces, suits, and ties lurked in the audience. These same gray men were imported into the second painting on the landing. It was a fanciful composition, showing Molly singing in a forest clearing, nude except for strategically curled flowers and green tendrils. The gray men buzzed around her on tweedy wings. One intrepid, delicate man was on the verge of flying into her open mouth—which was exaggerated in size and cushioned by her tongue and the vibrating nubs of her vocal cords. The third painting troubled me the most, in part because it was the last I saw on the way to the bedroom each night. It was a more restrained and realist interior painting of Molly in her dressing room. She sat before a lightbulb-edged mirror, applying lipstick. Reflected in the mirror alongside her was the familiar gray-faced and gray-suited man, but the composition of the painting made it unclear whether he was in fact looming behind her—or if he was the image she saw when she looked in the mirror.

THE DAY AFTER Kyle finished eleventh grade, we dragged the old Ping-Pong table in from the garage. We broke cobwebs, ragged it off, and eased it through the front door. Breathing heavily, we lingered in the foyer.

"We can put it by the piano," Kyle said. "Which I'm quitting."

"You are not," I replied, without conviction.

"I sucked," he said. "You know I sucked."

We slid the piano stool under the Steinway and moved it against the wall. I unclasped the stiff legs of the Ping-Pong table and killed a couple of spiders who'd nested, fat with eggs, in the joints. We admired the salvaged table, its boyish incongruity in the otherwise orderly room, then took up our paddles. Molly had always been in charge of Kyle's serious pursuits, school and piano, while the games were left to me. I related to him best as a competitor. My opponent across the table was hooded and obscure, clad in the same black sweatshirt he'd worn for most of the past year. Faint psoriasis scars lined his cheeks like the well-worn folds of a favorite letter, leaving a drift of skin flakes across his side of the table.

Our games were tense and silent, the only dialogue a laconic recital of scores and an occasional muttered "nice shot." The ball clapped through the house. Kyle had developed an unhittable return slam since the last time we'd played. There was a soft malevolence to it, but I didn't mind losing. A missed ball rolling down the floorboards reminded me of those marbles Kyle had rolled when he was younger. It must have reminded him too. He must have missed the sound of his mother's voice scolding us. When I looked up, the ash white and weightless ball in my palm, I found my opponent bent over the table, the hood drawn over his face completely.

"Listen, kid," I said. "I'm sorry. I'm sorry that I couldn't find your mother."

"Dad?"

He gave me a look I hadn't seen since he was a child, when he'd tried to phrase an existential question that was nagging his mind. It was a look of both doubt and trust—a pinched, imploring look.

"Yes?"

"Don't call me that," he said.

"Don't call you what?"

He sighed. "I ordered pizza on your credit card every night for three weeks."

"It's okay," I said. "I took out the boxes."

I edged past the net, clapped a paternal hand on his shoulder, then withdrew it.

THE BROCHURE TURNED up in our mailbox a few days later. I hardly even noticed its arrival. I could have torn it up right then, brought it to work and shredded it, unloaded it on our neighbors, but it didn't occur to me to do any of those things. I didn't stop Kyle from seeing it, and it reemerged in the center of the kitchen table, where it stayed, because no one was cleaning.

Greasy thumbprints appeared in the margins, nacho-powdered evidence of Kyle's close reading. It was nothing to me then, just another unrequested mailing from a church.

The story, rendered in graphic panels, followed a bewildered teen through a post-Rapture landscape of crashed airplanes and stalled traffic. The missing were everywhere, the shed skin of their rumpled clothes their only residue on a sidewalk or between the painted lines of a crosswalk. *He thought none of that God stuff mattered anymore, that he could do what he wanted.* I was on the verge of throwing it away, but for some reason I couldn't, weakened in my convictions. *The others were redeemed, but he's still here.* On the pamphlet's final page, the abandoned teen fell to his knees and cried. "Why didn't I pay attention in church? Why did I have premarital sex?" he implausibly exclaimed, while far above the ruined city, smoke gathered to form the features of a mournful savior. A huge horned beast was rising out of a distant lake. The final caption read, *If only he had opened his heart.*

The return address was a church on the I-99 frontage road, about two miles from our house. I'd been oblivious as I passed it every night on my way downtown from the office. At that hour, the exit for the church was as invisible to me as the exit for my own home. On that dusky drive, all I saw was my wife's face and the imagined face of her abductor, generic as a police sketch, but as solid as the pavement beneath me and the wheel in my hands.

3

I BROUGHT THE BROCHURE TO MY MOTHER THE NEXT TIME I went to see her at the Traumhaus. I'd been going there three times a week since Molly vanished, the way others might work out, and I always felt better afterward. There was something enormously consoling about the phrase "assisted living."

The Traumhaus had been designed by the Austrian émigré architect Klaus Bernhard. This eccentric and irascible man was responsible for several of Trude's landmarks, including the notorious Ringstrasse Mall, but the Traumhaus, a late work, was his most widely admired. It was on the outskirts of Trude. Leaving I-99 at the exit marked ARCHITECT'S END, a narrow paved road led you through several acres of pines and birches. At the edge of the property, the home was reflected in a pond where wooden ducks floated, a lifelike gloss on their feathers. Tricks of light and water made the reflected Traumhaus appear as a castle, replete with turrets and gargoyles. As you rounded the bend, then, the home's modernist steel-and-glass spareness came as a shock. The building seemed to float slightly above the landscape—a tenuous place, caught between worlds. Bernhard, who hated Trude, modeled the Traumhaus on a sanatorium that had loomed over his childhood village. But Europe was only in the reflection of the Midwestern pond with its fake ducks. Trude's most famous architect wished all his life to be elsewhere.

On some level I knew my mother wouldn't have many answers for me. She had some insight into single parenthood, but her mind was going, as they say, though this implies some sort of destination. She was better on the distant past than the recent past—"recent" being about fifteen years ago. Still, she was the only confidante I had then. I parked in the spacious lot of the Traumhaus, passed through the automatic doors, and approached the steel staircase. Mirrored on all sides, I climbed with my doppelgangers. Bernhard gazed down on me through thick-rimmed glasses from his portrait on the landing, a trace of amusement on his lips.

My mother waited over a Scrabble board in the Wittgenstein Lounge. Several framed prints of the letter *S* in plain serif hung around the room. I'd questioned a longtime Traumhaus resident about these prints, and she told me, in a whisper, that they were the work of the current occupant of the Schreber Suite. An abode of "unfathomable beauty," she said, although this was hearsay, because no one had ever been to the fourth floor; there was not even a button for it on the elevators. The prints were excerpts from memoirs written by the current occupant in the mid-eighties. They were widely studied. As to what the pages signified, there were competing theories. Some had suggested that the *S* stood for "sensation," or "senility," or "suffering." Others posited that the *S* was simply the first initial of the current occupant's name. He or she had not been seen in any of the common areas of the Traumhaus since Bernhard himself had vacated the Schreber Suite in 1983. "Only one thing is certain," the woman told me. "This writer has found a language of maximum power, compression, and elegance, which we are all trying to emulate in our own memoirs, although we inevitably fail."

My mother wore her best purple blouse and dark lipstick, her silver hair pulled into a bun. She was in great physical shape at seventy-two, and I sometimes wondered, given my penchant for self-abuse, whether she would outlive me. She hadn't dressed up for nothing. A dozen residents waited in Eames chairs as a few stragglers wheeled themselves in to watch. Evenings were a slow time at the Traumhaus. Harris sat in his usual chair next to her, buttoned up in a three-piece linen suit and a black beret. Wrinkled didn't begin to describe Harris's face. It was grooved, gouged, with two alarming white smears of eyebrow. This eighty-year-old aspiring silent comedian, who hadn't uttered a word in four years, was trying to seduce my mother.

"Hello, Sven," my mother said. "How is Molly?"

"She's great, Mom," I replied, wincing. "Busy as always."

I handed her the brochure. It was something I did, providing stimuli and letting her respond. It often surprised me, what an object would inspire her to say. The thing—a peach, a pencil sharpener—could get her reminiscing about the distant past, recalling characters and events from her childhood with a clarity that astonished me. Lately, though, I'd begun to suspect that these memories were contaminated with fiction, an especially troubling thought when the stories concerned my own early life. There was, for example, the story of my birth. Her recent retellings were peopled with new characters and more densely plotted, somehow. *You just didn't want to come out, you liked it so much in there*, she always began—and it was a good first line—but where did that poker-playing couple from Munich come in? And the friendly Italian nurse named Carlotta?

She removed her reading glasses from the collar of her blouse. She scrutinized the burning city and the locust clouds, then glanced at me. My mother had a kind of riflescope of concern, still functioning perfectly well. She fixed me in it.

"Those are Kyle's fingerprints," I said. "He was looking at it. But I can't say how interested he was. Maybe I'm overreacting."

She flipped a page. "Kyle . . . I know the name . . ." She gave a look I call the Bluff, a false dawning recognition. With my mother it was movement in the brow, indrawn breath, prayerful nodding. Everyone at the Traumhaus did some version of it.

"Your grandson."

"Of course, forgive me." She handed back the brochure. I gave her the bag of Scrabble tiles, which she dug into with her eyes closed. "Don't cheat, like you used to," she said.

I wasn't sure what she was referring to. As usual, I was overmatched. Her vocabulary hadn't suffered, and she jumped out to an early fifty point lead. Leaning on his cane, Harris nodded at my mother's formulations and shook his head at each of mine. It was a partisan crowd. My mother played her elegant, old-fashioned words to enthusiastic applause. Age having its way with youth, or relative youth at least—perhaps that's what they came to see.

After staring at my row of vowels, I played *oil*, which she quickly built into *tawny* and *toil*.

"The man who baptized you had sticky fingers."

I nodded. I managed *ion*.

"Yes, I remember it now," she said. "When he shook my hand, his fingers were sticky. He'd just come up from the basement. You know Lutherans, can't keep their hands off anything glazed. But you'd think he would wash up, don't you, before a baptism? His name was Grundquist, I believe. Some sort of sub-pastor."

Grundquist was something I could go on, a fact I could take out into the verifiable world.

"Did I ever tell you about the strange thing that happened during your baptism?" she asked. I blushed, but my mother basked in the attention. Her memoirs were highly regarded in this place; a few of her fellow residents scooted their chairs closer to listen.

I shook my head. "It's your turn," I said.

"This street person came into the church. Right as this Grundquist was reading the rite. He was tall, and he had wild hair, and a long beard with chunks of things in it. Like he'd just been eating stew with his face too close to the bowl." A respectful hush filled the lounge. An attendant paused in the hall, clipboard under her arm. Harris was jotting down my mother's words on a legal pad. I saw the man coming through the church doors. Saw the man in my mother's tale trying to dunk his head in the baptismal font. "It took two acolytes to restrain him," she went on. "Your father enjoyed it very much."

As if to underline her story, she played *brusque* across a double word score. Someone said, "Good heavens." A crutch dropped, others sighed with delight, and this seemed to be a response to the game and the story at once. I found myself parsing my mother's stories. I kept some details and discarded others. I let the absurd street person with the dirty beard wander back into the crannies of my mother's mind, but kept the sub-pastor with the sticky fingers.

Laying *pleb*, I tried another approach. "Let's say I wanted to get involved with a group of people with questionable beliefs."

"All right," she said warily.

"Possibly dangerous beliefs. What would you do?"

She built *despite* off *gourds* and paused until I was about to repeat the question. "Well, Sven," she said. "That would depend."

"On what?"

"It would depend," she said, "on whether I thought they could hurt you."

Harris nodded supportively, as if she'd stated his exact theory of parenthood. The gentle Harris struck me as a man who'd once been violent, a guy who had dwindled into his own opposite. Maybe it was the suits, which looked to have been tailored for a larger, more threatening man.

"What if it wasn't a question of getting hurt so much?"

I was losing her. She wiped her spectacles as if one final scrub of the glass would make the world clear.

"What if it was a matter of being led astray. Into a kind of delusion. A dubious alternate reality."

"I'm sorry. Dubious? What was the question now?"

I reached for her hand across the table. "Never mind, it doesn't matter."

"I wish I could keep better track of these things," she said. Her eyes flickered across her rack of letters. "You didn't cheat while I was wiping my glasses, right?"

"No, Mom," I said. "I didn't cheat."

Mom looked to Harris. In order to maintain his vow of silence, Harris kept a small green chalkboard dangling around his neck at all times. He removed a slab of chalk from his coat pocket and, after bobbling it a little for the amusement of the crowd, scratched out his verdict and turned it to my mother. "He didn't cheat," it read, "and I would never lie to you."

The bag was depleted, but I had drawn good tiles. The letters did not spell out disaster, and there were still some things I could control. Luckily, I had an *S*. I found *pains*, then *panics*, then searched the board for an opening to deliver my unlikely coup de grace: *escaping*.

4

I DID GET THAT CALL FROM DETECTIVE MCCREADY AT TRUDE'S tenth precinct station, to my surprise. It came three months after Molly's disappearance, almost to the day. He called me at work. The law office of my employer, William S. Boggs, was located in a strip mall off I-99 "in the glow of Rip's Sporting Goods," as the commercials put it. It had been a slow afternoon in personal injury. Our only remaining client of the day was an eye-patched man wearing two sweatshirts despite the summer heat. He squinted through his good eye at one of the gentlemen's magazines Boggs subscribed to. I'd seen women glance uncomfortably in their direction and didn't really consider them good lobby fare, but that was one of many battles I'd lost long ago.

"Good afternoon," I answered. "Office of Boggs, tell us where it hurts."

The detective informed me that there had been a development in my wife's case. The force had acquired a document whose significance was not yet clear, but they were pretty sure—

near certain, he stressed—that it pertained to Molly's disappearance. I goaded him for more information, but he insisted that I read it for myself. Could I come down to the station right away?

I knocked on the door of Boggs's lair. A crisp file was spread out on his formidable mahogany desk. He stood at the large industrial paper shredder against the back wall, feeding documents into its maw. As he did this, he gazed out at the row of parked cars behind the strip mall. He gestured me in with a barely perceptible flick of his pointer finger. My employer, a minor celebrity in Trude on account of his late-night cable TV ads, was a man of great physical beauty. He was tall, broad-shouldered, and wore exquisitely tailored pinstripe suits that accentuated his dignified salt-and-pepper hair. His chin was firm, his hands soft and sinuous. These hands, with their subtle, liquid acquisitiveness, must have played a part in his astonishing success with women. (A note on Boggs's hands: I had tracked down several Shaker chairs and Edwardian sideboards to placate Boggs's antique-collecting wife, Sheila, after she'd discovered one of his affairs. At one point, Sheila invited me to the Boggsian home for dinner. As Boggs led me on a "house tour," he caressed these objects as if reliving the affairs they represented.)

He turned to me, rubbing his hands together softly. I explained the phone call and asked if I could have the rest of the afternoon off.

"By all means," he said, sliding into his chair and swiveling up to the desk. "If you think that is a good idea."

"A good idea?" I asked.

Boggs smiled thinly. I was close enough to the man to know that he never uttered a careless word. In court, he often couched his most devastating points within seemingly irrelevant digressions. "Bewilderment is a precious commodity, Nor-berg," he said. He caught me in his gaze. His eyes were his most deceptive gift. The film guys had recognized this, shooting the ads in claustrophobic close-up. Boggs's eyes, which accord-ing to the cliché ought to have been windows on a shuddering, black void, were instead two orbs of enigmatic hazel. Eyes of a minor deity who looked upon human events with interest and compassion and longed to intervene. *You deserve justice, justice, justice*, they cried.

"With all due respect," I said, "I think that is somewhat facile, sir."

"Of course it is," he replied. "I just wanted you to stop and think. To consider the perfect ignorance in which you find your-self. But by all means, go, pursue this. The collation can wait until morning."

I mentioned the eye-patched man who had been waiting through Boggs's hour-and-fifteen-minute lunch.

"Tell him to come back tomorrow," said Boggs. "I'm not in the mood."

I went. "Mr. Boggs is indisposed," I told the client. He ac-cepted this with a meek shrug and trailed me out of the office. I got in my car and whistled westbound on I-99, the windows open to the languorous midsummer air. I had not been down-town since my nights of painful and fruitless sleuthing. In sun-light, the buildings lost their malice and threat—I could see their peeling paint, their rusting ironwork and dim palimpsests. WACKER AND SONS: FOR A REAL SHINE, THE TIME IS RIGHT FOR SQUIBB'S COLA. The aged high-rises comforted me in their half-wrecked, almost fleshly failings. I parked in a line of vacant meters across from the tenth precinct station. The neighborhood was quiet. Two men in bowler hats were making a suspect transaction in an alley, and a woman cried "Sparky, stop that!" at a creature I could not locate.

Passing through the familiar double doors, I found cops playing chess, cops dozing beside whirring fans, cops reading thick ex-library books—picked up on the cheap at one of the Central Library's recent liquidation sales, I supposed. I asked for McCready at the front desk. The receptionist's book bag, crumpled next to her chair, was a different-colored version of the one Molly had carried her sheet music in. She pointed to McCready's open door before picking up where she'd left off in *Fear and Trembling*. Inside, McCready was at his desk, exhaling a ragged line of pipe smoke. His appearance had changed. He wore a neat brown beard and horn-rimmed glasses. A tweed coat hung over the back of his chair, complementing the framed portrait of Wittgenstein. The new look fit him so well that I found it difficult to remember what he'd looked like before.

"Mr. Norberg," he said. "I apologize for the long delay. This has been a very vexing case for me. I spent a few days in the hospital with a heart murmur, nothing serious. They tell me it was psychosomatic."

"I see." I nodded, coughing. The room was incredibly smoky.

"Have you met my colleague?"

A young man with slicked-back blond hair and racer shades rolled out from behind a file cabinet. He wore an unseasonal argyle sweater vest and nodded behind a smoldering cigarillo.

"We call him 'the Oracle' around here," said McCready. "Because he doesn't talk much. But when he does, you can bet it will be profound."

The Oracle nodded sagely.

"Down to business, then," said McCready. "I'd like to hear your reading of this document." He handed me a manila folder with two typewritten pages inside. The pages were grubby and coffee-stained. Commentary in at least two different illegible hands lined the margins.

CONFESSION OF JIMENEZ

You ask, why was I pursuing the athletic Lenya Leskovich across the tennis clay. Well, sirs, I answer. I am a major fan of hers from long ago. Do I pursue other females? No sirs, I do not. Only she can be saving me, <u>my only Lenya Leskovich. You</u> have troubled me, I will explain.

I was dwelling in a number 9 house many miles from your city. I trust you know what I am speaking. My madre, my brothers, my sisters and also half-sisters, and also my Uncle Pedro lived in this house. It was very cramping. The ceiling was holy. <u>Many other little leaks, yes.</u>

I obtained unemployment checks by direct deposit so I had no needing to depart the number 9 house. I sat on the couch and became dolorous watching the TV program Hourglass. *My dolors became deep and I wanted to cry like the females on this program. Then one day I flicked the channel and I witnessed Lenya Leskovich swinging the racket. Her tennis costume was inspiring to me. I knew that Lenya was the most beautiful virgin I had witnessed.*

It is no secret that I get busy with many females, and <u>many other long-legged youths</u>. Members of my posse say I am like a Don Giovanni because I shake so many mattresses. <u>My organ is large like a yam</u>. Let those who have ears to hear, hear.

What is so hot about females and virgins swinging the racket?

When Lenya Leskovich shoots her first and second serves, she makes a very beautiful sound. This sound she makes is like "uhh," but it is also like "Oh, Jimenez! I am enjoying what you do to me very much!" I made records of Lenya's games with the video machine. Yet I remained dolorous. I could not find proper enjoyment of my video records. My life was a <u>misery of little, lost yearnings</u>.

When I learned that Lenya would be swinging the racket in your city, I traveled there on a cramping bus and obtained a ticket to Lenya's tennis game against the old female Katja Bjornsen of Norway.

I hoped for my conference with Lenya to be joyful. However, when I ran into the tennis clay, Lenya was ruminating ways to defeat the old female from Norway, and she did not spy me. "My only love, Lenya, you—" I uttered, but I was muffled by tackling guards, and she did not understand my speaking. I only witnessed Lenya's ankles from the clay. I knew that her ankles were the making of God. Only God can make a beautiful virgin. I will find Lenya again. I know this. I will see her, even if I am locked in for a <u>multitude of long, lonely years</u>.

MCCREADY RELIT HIS pipe. "Well?"

"I'm a little unclear on the significance of this," I said.

McCready glanced at the Oracle, who nodded over his glinting shades.

"The code," McCready said.

"Pardon?"

"The encoded name in the confession," said McCready impatiently. He removed his horn rims and scrubbed them with the tail of his shirt. "'Many other little leaks, yes.' 'Many other long-legged youths.'"

"'My organ,'" the Oracle quoted, "'is large—'"

"Yes. Must we spell it out for you, Norberg?"

"Molly," I said. I reread the underlined portions of the confession with a chill. For a long, superstitious moment, I was convinced.

"This is clearly the work of a devious mind," mused McCready. "This banal confession of tenniphilia, if you'll permit the coinage, may mask a subtext of true guilt. As we read and reread the confession, I thought, 'I remember that sad little fellow who used to come in here every night, looking for his wife.'"

"I have been reading your wife's file very closely," the Oracle said, pressing his fingers to his temple. "Her name is very much on my mind."

"As we discussed your wife," McCready continued, dragging a wispy wraith of smoke around the room, almost as if he were dancing with it, "my colleague recalled that he had seen her in a production of *Don Giovanni*, which Jimenez references in his confession."

With McCready's pipe and the Oracle's cigarillo going full blaze, I decided to light a cigarette myself. Amid the thick smoke, we were like three neophytes at a séance. I contemplated the text in my hands. "Aren't we reading too much into this?" I asked.

McCready pulled on his pipe, nonplussed. The Oracle wheeled over.

"After all," I said, "Jimenez is a man who draws a distinction between 'females' and 'virgins.' The so-called code could be accidental—or it might mean something entirely different than you've supposed. As for the Mozart reference, that's a mistake. He clearly means to say 'Don Juan' there."

The Oracle leaned back. "We find it profitable," he said, "to treat mistakes as buried intentions."

"Where is Jimenez?" I asked. "Have you questioned him?"

The two detectives shared a pained look. McCready said, "You may have heard about the new mayor's passion for budget cutting. We've lost some of our best officers. Regrettably, Jimenez escaped. Do let us know if you run into him."

"But how would I recognize him?"

There was a pause, the heavy silence of the Oracle in thought. "You would know him," the Oracle said finally, "by his manner of speaking."

McCready stroked his beard. "Norberg may have a point," he conceded. "Perhaps our methods have become too refined. Perhaps we have misunderstood this confession of Jimenez."

I turned to the Oracle. His hands lay like unsent letters in his lap. His preternatural calm unnerved me. "You saw my wife in *Don Giovanni*?"

He took a patient pull on his cigarillo, savored its gradual burn. He was in no hurry to speak as McCready paced the room and I tapped my foot nervously.

"Indeed. I was privileged to hear her famous performance in the tenor role of Don Ottavio."

I was woozy with smoke. Molly had never told me about this feat. Though with her incredible range, I did not doubt her ability to sing a male part. The words of Jimenez atomized, scattered characters trembling on the page before me.

"When was this?"

"The last performance of last season," the Oracle said. "You mean, you didn't know? You didn't read the reviews? Martin Breeze called it, I believe, the most impressive vocal feat—"

"No," I interrupted. "I tried to avoid Molly's reviews. 'The sumptuous Molly Norberg.' 'The fetching Molly Norberg.' They always made me jealous." I handed McCready the manila folder and rose from my chair. "Well, thanks for thinking of me," I said, halfway out of the room already. "Do keep her in mind."

"Of course," McCready said. "Though I think we should be thanking you, Norberg. You've shown us that we need to take a more basic approach."

"Like the fundamentalists," the Oracle added. An ironic smile twisted his lips. "The word means what it says, and says what it means." McCready, flopping in his chair, looked disappointed with this tautology.

The dark beam of the Oracle's stare remained on me. "I hope your quest ends well," he said, exhaling a curl of smoke. "I hope you are more successful than our friend Jimenez." And he pushed the shades back over the bridge of his nose.

I WANDERED OUT into the muggy, landlocked heat of August. The sun was boiling and relentless; flies capsized in a sweet grave of warm soda at my feet. I did not contemplate what the word "fundamentalist" might mean, coming from the mouth of an Oracle. It was hard to even think about Molly. I thought of the Don in a tight frock chirping about his 1,002 conquests in Italy or whatever. I passed the block of the Opera House. It was the architect Bernhard's first major project in Trude, and he came to consider it a conservative, gaudy failure. Yet those gargoyles and chandeliers still drew crowds. Even now the cars were rolling in for the matinee. The people of Trude had a taste for opera; my wife had done well here. I stopped at the corner where I'd turned so many times to trace her steps, then forced myself to walk away.

I followed Hamsun Avenue down to the Central Library. A beaux arts palace with high arched windows and two gilded owls whose eyes had once glowed in the dark flanking its front staircase. The owls' eyes had closed with the brass gates. It was now a tense disputed zone. Our new mayor, Dwight "the Fist" Fuller, had coasted to landslide on a histrionic and brutal budget reform plan. A decorated veteran and an ex–pro wrestler who had sparred with the likes of Jerome the Jackal and the Non-Amigo, Fuller had turned his violent energies against the city's bloated and antiquated infrastructure. His inaugural address began: "Citizens of Trude, we have become a sickly, namby-pamby people. Too effete and decadent by far. Think about it— what are we known for? Our mental asylum, our shopping mall, and *opera*." In his first days of office, Fuller pummeled the Historic Preservation Board, the Forestry Department, the Complaint Desk. The Beautification Bureau found itself exiled from its crumbling office suite. But he wasn't done. He slashed public library budgets so deeply that they were forced to sell off their rare books, their extensive holdings of city records, their bound medical and legal periodicals (Boggs had bought a set of these), and, finally, large portions of the circulating collection. Amid layoffs and emergency book sales, it became clear that Fuller intended not a bureaucratic overhaul, but a complete starvation of the public library system. The neighborhood branches soon closed, followed by the larger regional branches. Outraged editorials were printed and ignored. When Fuller announced a second round of closings, the remaining librarians organized and took refuge at Central. Availing themselves of newly liberalized gun laws, they formed a small militia, which for a time kept the peace while maintaining access to the stacks. Now, however, Fuller's demolition team had moved in, buffeted by a handful of police. The police, smarting from salary and pension cuts, and the loss of the annual Policemen's Ball, were more ambivalent than the mayor expected. They refused to raid the library. This civic crisis had reached a standstill by midsummer.

Roadblocks were up now, and the street was full of loitering men in orange flak jackets and library patrons irrationally waiting for the building to reopen. Traffic cops strolled the scene, sipping coffee from white paper cups. A heavy wrecking ball dangled from a crane and rocked slowly over the street. Police tape festooned the grounds, though it was unclear what the tape demarcated exactly. Pigeons strutted the cobblestones, browsing for muffin and croissant crumbs. Librarians loomed in the high arched windows. Their watchful lenses caught shards of sunlight. I felt for them, these formerly mild public servants, driven to rage. Guardians of the sensible world, they had been assailed by a dark force, and who could blame them for taking up arms against it? Two gray-haired women stood on either end of the palatial front staircase, flanked by the blind golden owls. Their dignity was immense. They wore Hush Puppies. They held shotguns. If I hadn't a son to go home to, a son who I thought then *needed a father*, I would have joined them, those sentries, those last defenders of reason, order, and beauty.

5

K YLE'S SEVENTEENTH BIRTHDAY FELL IN MID-AUGUST, AND IN the days leading up to it I shopped for gifts and confections. As if I could plaster over the rift that was already growing between us with wrapping paper, ribbons, and frosting. I'd had plenty of chances to consider my shortcomings as a parent, waking on the couch in my work clothes among the littered remnants of last night's wine and cigarettes. I needed to call some people. I excavated the numbers of neighbors and opera friends from Molly's bulging address book. I even put in a call to Boggs, who had four lovely daughters. All four of them picked up at once (they had a "party line"), but when I mentioned Kyle's name, they conjured maladies, summer school projects, a distant family reunion. As it turned out, there was a lot happening on August 12. The pretexts piled up as my invitations were declined. Some pall of disaster had fallen over us. Frau Huber alone was delighted to come and promised to bring a batch of her famous nut balls.

Over white takeout boxes from Li Po's—a sizable colony of which had formed on the kitchen counter—I asked Kyle who else he'd like to invite, and strongly implied that I would be willing to buy beer.

He lowered his eyes. "You must think I have friends or something."

"Sure you do," I said. "Don't you?" I added, realizing that I would be hard-pressed to name one. "Kids from school?"

"School's out," Kyle said.

"I am aware, but back when I was your age, we sometimes picked up the phone and—"

"Just forget it, okay?" He had mauled the chicken with his fork and was now raking white rice over the remains. "I don't even want to think about school until you make me go back. You should have heard the things they said about Mom."

"Are you serious?"

"They said . . . that she was a slut and probably went to France, because that's where they invented the threesome."

"Idiots," I said, lighting a mid-meal smoke.

"So if it's all right with you, let's just skip the party. I'm not in the party mood, to be perfectly honest, Dad."

"It is *not* all right with me. But if you want, we can do something quiet. Mrs. Huber is coming, and I'm still waiting to hear from a couple people."

"Mrs. Huber, great," Kyle said, planting his fork. He narrowed his eyes at me. "Mom would be pissed if she knew you were smoking at the table."

"Well," I replied, "she's not here, is she."

FRAU HUBER ARRIVED an hour early, holding a cookie tin embossed with a blue windmill and an envelope inscribed to

Kyle in a shaky hand. She wore an ancient mauve party dress with a clump of cat hair dangling from the sleeve. For several years I'd been urging Molly to break off the so-called lessons with Frau Huber. "I couldn't do it," Molly always said. "She would have nothing." The old lady was adrift in our living room and I guided her toward an armchair.

"We're glad you're here," I said. Playing the gracious host, I put on water for tea. As the water boiled, I casually mentioned my recent conversation with the Oracle at the tenth precinct station.

"Strange, isn't it, that Molly never told me about that performance."

"She was always so modest," Huber replied elusively. "Yet it is strange. It was a major triumph for her—no more than a handful of mezzos in the world could have handled that role. Just a little milk, please." Huber seemed grateful for the distraction of the spoon and sugar, avoiding my gaze. "Imagine that, the tenor and his understudy being ill on the same night!"

I nodded at Frau Huber without smiling. "I have to go out," I said. It was true. Huber's resemblance to an aged and frail Molly was too unsettling to endure for long intervals. This wasn't going to be much of a party, it was painfully clear. Would it have been so much for Boggs to let me borrow a couple of his daughters for the afternoon? Couldn't someone have skipped a doubles match or a dress rehearsal?

I climbed into Molly's car, feeling buzzed, untrustworthy, humming to myself. It was hard to wring much sense of occasion from the ashen sky, my brain fuzzed by last night's alcohol or today's.

The bakery, when I reached it, was closing. Like many of

the neighborhood businesses this seemed to be its default position. The neighborhood historian, a reclusive chain smoker, had told me the building was once a philosophical academy devoted to Hegelian and Marxist thought. It now offered a murky dialectic of bakery and chop suey stand, and a superstructure of boarded windows.

"Hang on," I called to the clerk, still rattling her keys in the bakery door.

She turned, and I had the odd sense of being truly noticed. Not just regarded or acknowledged, but seen. The girl had very large eyes. She had a metal stud in her left nostril and a blue streak in her short brown hair.

"Oh," she said. "I'd given up hope on you."

I glanced at the spot on my wrist where a watch might have been. "I must have lost track of time."

She was already reopening the door. "It's just that we've been getting a lot of strange orders lately," she said. "People are paying for cakes in advance but not coming to pick them up. I don't get it. The owner wants to rename the shop Cake for Cake's Sake." She rolled her eyes. "And yes, before you ask, I do eat some of the unclaimed cakes. I guess that's obvious."

"Not to me."

"That's a nice thing to say to a fat girl."

It was sitting there alone in the display case. *For a singular son at seventeen* was written in blue frosting on the white cake, faintly colored by the light from a high stained glass window. Across the counter, the girl was fishing for my invoice. She didn't look fat to me, but I hadn't been an especially harsh critic of appearances lately. Boggs had called my own look "Dostoevskian" the other day.

"Did you do the frosting?" I asked.

"Yeah, that's me, I do all the inscriptions."

"It's beautiful," I said. "I didn't think people learned to write cursive that way anymore." And I was thinking of letters Molly had written me in college, while she was studying abroad. Her spidery, looping script had seemed like an extension of her gentle, distant hand. The way the two *L*s had hooked into the *Y* like a line of thread that just happened to fall that way.

From the way the girl read the invoice, I could tell that she'd heard the news. My name had become a diagnosis. I thanked her and carried the cake to the car.

Inside, I rested my head against the seat and lit a cigarette. When the smoke cleared she was standing at the bus stop, leaning forward on her high-top sneakers and peering down the vast wrecked corridor of the boulevard. Then she slumped back on the sagging bench, next to the eroded headshot of a real estate agent. When I saw a Trude bus it was usually steaming with its hazards on. I didn't want to leave her alone; there had been shootings in the area, though it was now eerily still.

I rolled down the window. "I could take you somewhere," I called. "If you don't mind stopping by my son's birthday party first."

For a moment she seemed to consider the street's dangers and her misgivings about the guy behind the wheel. It was not an easy choice she faced, far from it. I kept my eyes fixed on the street until I heard the door and felt the weight shift in the car. Reaching down for the shift, my hand landed next to the red, swollen knob of her knee, which showed through her torn tights.

"I tripped," she said. "I haven't figured out how to walk in these boots."

Her name, she told me, was Plea. Her full name was Pleiades, after the constellation. Her parents weren't around: they were at a swingers' convention in Omaha for the weekend, she said. As we drove, she freshened her lipstick in the passenger mirror, and it felt good to see someone do that again.

BY THE TIME we returned home, Kyle was in bed. A parallelogram of murky light from the tiny basement window landed on his midriff. He looked like he was slowly becoming part of the foundation. A song crashed through the headphones inside his hood. To reach up, to extract the headphones from the ears, to verify the cause of the disturbance—it was a major effort, and he looked at me with deep fatigue. I guided the birthday boy upstairs, where Plea and Frau Huber were having an awkward tête-à-tête over the untouched cookie tin. "Basically, I just sing in the shower," Plea was saying. "Where the acoustics are good and no one will hear me."

Kyle emerged to ground level blinking at the two women. He looked affronted by all the food and wrapped gifts. Frau Huber enveloped him in her menthol embrace. "Happy birthday, my son," she said, weirdly. The hug extended way beyond its appropriate length until I realized that Frau Huber was crying on Kyle's sweatshirt sleeve. Arms clamped to his sides, he glared at me over Huber's shoulder. I still had not introduced him to the girl.

"Kyle, I want you to meet Plea," I said, peeling off Frau Huber. "We met at the bakery and I thought you two might get along. I think she actually goes to your school." I took Frau Huber to the kitchen and poured her some wine. She apologized all the way: there were certain things she couldn't understand. She was so old-fashioned and a young man like that ought to have his mother, she said. I told her that I agreed entirely. The wine was a nice Burgundy—I was making inroads into the more expensive precincts of our cellar now—and it seemed to steady her somewhat. I wanted to tell her that her words were tearing into my chest, but instead I reminded her that we were trying to have a good time and that no one wanted to talk about Molly.

"Of course, you are right," she said. "I will behave better."

Back in the family room, Plea was sitting next to Kyle on the couch and running the back of her hand along the side of his cheek. Little flakes of his face landed on the black leather. It amazed me that he was letting her do it.

"It's really interesting," she said. "The way it feels."

"Well, are we ready for presents?" I asked.

Frau Huber's gift, as I'd feared, was piano-related—the sheet music for Schumann's Kinderszenen, a piece Molly had been urging on Kyle, though it was far too difficult for him. She had always overestimated his musical abilities . . . Kyle took a cursory look at the staffs, the key signature, the drizzle of notes, and grunted in the direction of Frau Huber. Perhaps she hadn't noticed the closed cover on the piano keyboard, the scrim of dust that had settled over it. Kyle was more receptive to the contents of the envelope, his eyes lighting up when he saw the sum on the check.

"Wow, thanks," he said.

Frau Huber nodded from Molly's antique rocker, colorless as a figure in a charcoal sketch. I was not sure how this impoverished voice coach could have the money to make large birthday donations, especially now that she'd lost her most accomplished student.

My own gifts for Kyle had been the product of long and tense deliberations. Never an efficient shopper, it was even harder now that I was on my own and the stakes seemed higher. Wandering the famously disorienting corridors of Bernhard's Ringstrasse Mall, I'd stayed until closing several nights, haunting the shops until the clerks sighed audibly. There were a couple of heavy metal CDs that I'd chosen because Martin Breeze, the music critic for the *Trumpet*, had singled them out in a column called Symptoms of Cultural Decline. A pair of sunglasses, which I hoped would remind Kyle of the relatively good times we'd had together as I taught him to drive. A new stereo, a sketchbook, a handful of gift cards: I knew that I had somehow fallen short. Molly had always been so good at finding joke gifts, those little grace notes: the stress ball, the robotic dog.

"I'm sorry I didn't get you anything," Plea said.

"It's okay." Kyle balled up some wrapping paper in his hand. "I mean, I just met you an hour ago."

I wouldn't have minded a thanks. I took it out on Frau Huber, who had been nibbling her cake slice quietly in the corner. She half-yawned, and I jumped at the opportunity to tell her how tired she must have been, how late it was. I shepherded her to the door, returning her tin of untouched nut balls. She insisted that I keep them, *she had made them especially for us*, she said with odd emphasis, adding that if there was anything at all she could do, anything in the house that needed a woman's touch, or if we wanted a home-cooked meal, we only had to ask. I thanked her, although I wouldn't be calling any time soon to request her heavy plates of sauerbraten and spaetzle.

"Of course, we will," I said, nearly pushing her out the door. As I closed her out the old woman's mouth opened, as if about to say something or sing a high note. After pausing a moment on the front step, she hobbled out to the bus stop. Though I felt guilty for not offering her a ride, I watched her go with incredible relief.

"What?" I asked the teens, who stared me down critically. "I think I forgot something," I said, climbing the stairs to collect Kyle's last present. I passed the painting of Molly singing in the coliseum. I passed the swarms of buzzing gray men, and the dim man in the mirror. I wondered if she would have approved of how I was handling the situation. No, I thought, she certainly wouldn't have. I lingered in the bedroom to smoke a cigarette. Our mattress was rumpled on my side, flat on Molly's—some superstition, or perhaps simply habit, had prevented me from crossing the central boundary. I listened to the murmur of voices from the room below. With the sigh of a swimmer prepared for a blast of cold water, I put out my cigarette and went to the closet. I dove behind Molly's dresses and, submerged in a wave of her scent, dug for the package. I carried it downstairs, making my slow steps as creaky as I could.

Kyle stared from his mound of wrapping paper and ribbons: he knew what it was. Molly and I had argued over it many times, she taking the hard-line position that it would erode his morals, attention span, and sense of reality; me making the laissez-faire point that the culture would get him sooner or later. He unwrapped it slowly and warily, the psoriasis scars on his cheeks like imprinted tears. The video game console was shiny and sleek. It gleamed in his hands.

"Maybe Plea would like to play a few games," I said.

"You know," she said, "all that food made me realize how tired I am. Maybe I could just crash out on the couch for a little while? Be as loud as you want. I can sleep anywhere."

"I'm glad you came," Kyle said shyly.

"You should thank your father," she said.

I sat down on the throw rug next to my son and picked up a controller. We stayed there for several hours, hardly speaking, as our hard-boiled avatars explored the world of *Bad Cops, No Badges*. The game involved driving through a nameless city, arresting criminals, molesting strippers, destroying trees, mailboxes, and traffic lights, stealing cars, shooting innocent civilians at point-blank range, and in short, inhabiting an anarchic universe (though the old moral order lingered fleetingly in the form of a dour church bell, which announced the departure of these virtual souls). My detective was prone to confusion and sometimes ended up running against a wall, slowed by wine and age, but on the whole I held my own. I veered, shot, battered, stole, destroyed, and every one of my victims was the man who had encountered Molly that evening in the city on her way to buy an egg, the man who saw her walking alone and figured, *hell, why not*. I pounded the controller until my thumbs hurt, but it did not diminish the void in my heart. When there was a pause in the action, from time to time, I heard Plea breathing on the couch behind us. She was still there when I went upstairs and Kyle went down, but in the morning she was gone, leaving only a napkin with some bagel crumbs on it.

IT IS HARD to remember much more about that summer. I could report on the slow churning of the ceiling fan, and my pursuit of Molly-shaped phantoms across the damp sheets, but the only salient fact about those delirious months was that they ended.

When the heat haze lifted, it was time for Kyle to start classes at Humboldt High, and we went back to school shopping at the mall. Kyle deserved things, I felt, in lieu of justice. Enough consumer goods might distract us from the mausoleum-like hush of the house at night. I gave him twenty or thirty bucks and let him wander that forest of shrink-wrapped objects. At that point I didn't realize exactly how close the mall was to the First Church of the Divine Purpose, because they hadn't yet built the three giant crosses that made it so visible from the road.

We wandered its chambers and antechambers, its circles of insanely specialized stores, such as Little = Cute (every item less than two inches in diameter), the Ping-Pong Palace, Remember the Crucifixion?, So Many Cookies . . . , and After Nature. The mall's spiral design was called "totalitarian" by Bernhard's detractors—a sizable contingent in Trude. There was really only one way to walk the mall: by starting at the outer ring, which housed the larger department stores. Working inward, through a series of nested circular arcades, the big stores gave way to niche shops, and the innermost rings resembled street markets, with merchants, artisans, and charlatans selling their wares from crammed tables. At the very center of the mall stood a labyrinth of tall hedges—as if the mall wanted to be, at its heart, a cathedral or a seminary. Bernhard left very specific instructions for the maintenance of these hedges. They were flooded, eerily, with fluorescent track lighting and watered from above by spigots that turned on every quarter hour. *There is a solution to the labyrinth*, Bernhard had cryptically uttered at the groundbreaking ceremony. That no one in thirty years had discovered it didn't stop others from trying. The mall had become Trude's most popular tourist attraction, despite its impracticality for actual shopping: people flew in from all over the world simply to walk through it, departing the city without even setting foot downtown. Maybe the ultimate emptiness at the heart of capitalism was the architect's didactic joke. They sold a souvenir T-shirt at a stand outside the labyrinth, screen-printed with Bernhard's spiral blueprint and the slogan TRUDE: WE TRIED.

Kyle's selections were surprising: polo shirts and khakis replaced the daily sweatshirt and jeans wardrobe of the year before. I assumed he was taking a newfound interest in the opposite sex. Meanwhile I paid a visit to the Bachelor's Library, curated by a balding, mustached fellow in dandruff-flecked tweed. I purchased two discs, *Indecent Reference* and *Card Catalog Confidential*. The latter was a rarity, its obsolescence only enhancing its appeal. I'd been relying on such discs for several years, as Molly had so often been absent at night, or on tour, or tired and hoarse. I needed something to cover the videos, so I treated myself to a leather jacket on clearance. I met Kyle by the wishing well. We wandered Bernhard's labyrinth, pleasantly burdened. The shopping bags had a nice heft.

"Is that a leather jacket?" Kyle asked on the way to the parking lot.

"Mm-hmm. Don't worry, I'm not even thinking about a convertible."

"Good," he said. "It's pretty cool."

"Want to drive?" I asked.

His driver's exam was coming up in a few weeks, and he was getting in as much practice as he could. Not that it was too difficult to get a license in Trude—it was actually much easier than getting a library card, since the library crisis had developed. I tossed him the keys. He grinned as he turned the ignition, confidently pressed the clutch, and backed out into the lot. I was amazed at how quickly he'd learned the manual transmission. He made swift, sure turns and navigated the highway with a proprietary ease. Though I had been unaware of it, he'd been watching me and learning from me all this time.

6

AVING NO GREATER CAUSE THAT SUNDAY, I LOADED THE OLD picnic basket with wine, bread, and cheese. I did this automatically, and was almost surprised to find myself, half an hour later, in the procession of couples heading to the Arcadia Pavilion for the last concert of the season. The folly was formed from the skeletal remains of century-old fairground arcades and was surrounded by the busts of romantic composers set on high poles, as if they were criminals who had been impaled there.

There was no problem finding room on the hillside. The night was humid and listless, totally unpleasant, and I had to congratulate myself on the fact that I'd stayed away from here all summer, forgoing many great concerts on beautiful evenings, because I couldn't really bear to attend without Molly, only to break down at the last minute, on this truly nasty night, to attend a program of Mozart symphonies.

* * *

EVERYTHING WAS THE same as always. The musicians were onstage tuning, a pit stain here and there amid the white dress shirts. The fountains murmured along with the couples breaking baguettes and smearing soft cheese. Turtles relaxed in the man-made pond. Kids traversed the hillside, testing the limits of their white wine induced freedom, weaving through the blankets, chasing the intermittent sparks of fireflies.

Everything the same, except. There was something unavoidably creepy about a guy alone on a picnic. Families and couples steered clear of me, creating a buffer zone around my musty blanket. Finally a hirsute exhibitionist, the kind of guy who finds any excuse to whip off his shirt—he probably hadn't even brought one—stopped just below me to take stock. He had a jutting forehead, unkempt blond curls, and mutton chops. Sweaty chest in full view, he surveyed the hill, acknowledging his intrusion into my personal space with a "hey bro." As I reached down to scratch a mosquito bite on my ankle, the first of many, my new neighbor ripped open a bag of barbeque chips.

Molly and I had come here almost every week back in the spaghetti days. We could hardly afford records at the time, and the concerts were free. We filled our picnic basket and sometimes waded in the fountains, Molly's red hair spilling over her dark green swimsuit and tangling in the cheap white frames of her drugstore sunglasses. When Kyle was a baby, it was our escape, once a month in the summer if we could afford the sitter. We came here and tried to pretend we weren't tired parents, ignoring echoes of our son's crying in the violins.

"You're going to the pavilion?" Kyle had asked earlier that night, seeing me alone at the front door with the basket. "You sure?"

I nodded without answering.

"Do you have bug spray?"

I told him I couldn't find it. "Mosquitoes don't like the taste of me," I said, and asked if he wanted to come along.

He paused his game, a citizen about to bite the dust. "No, I don't think so," he said deliberately, as if reading aloud in class. "I think it would be weird."

As in fact it was, and he'd had a point about the bug spray. My neighbor was slathering it on, adding a chemical sheen to his torso. The orchestra slogged through the slow movement of the night's first Mozart symphony, serenading the lowering cloud of hungry mosquitoes. They had always, quite understandably, preferred the taste of Molly. Now they settled for the remains.

WE HAD GONE to the pavilion the night Molly got back from New York all those years ago. When I'd taken her to the airport, five days before, she'd been effervescent and hopeful, singing chirpy bits of *Tosca* to the friends who'd come to see her off, everyone certain of her success. The Molly who got off the plane was humbled and veiled, sunglasses and an old lady's scarf over her hair. How could I explain the difference in my mood on these two occasions? During the send-off, as Molly sang and laughed, I was miserable, all too aware of my own glum irrelevance (which would only become more pronounced in the probable New York future). As Molly disembarked the plane in heavy disguise, I was here alone to drive her home, to comfort her, to cook her the spaghetti that she only ate in emergencies. Only I knew how to cook it right. I found myself once again a necessary Norberg. I trilled secretly. On the ride home I listened to the story of her nightmare audition, the pond of darkened faces down there among the plush cloth, the voice calling out "that's enough" with chill finality, out of that murky reddish darkness. I listened and nodded, murmured and consoled. When she had talked herself out I carried her luggage into the bedroom and put her to sleep. Later, I sat on the edge of the bed. She blinked, and I saw the innocence of sleep give way. Molly's irises clouded as she oriented herself in the Midwest, in Trude, and finally in the crappy one bedroom off Dead Mayor Boulevard where we were living in sin at the time.

"Let's get drunk," I said, stroking her cheek gently, as if I might smear her freckles.

"I can't go out, Norberg."

"Let's get drunk and go swimming."

She laughed, then cried again until her small frame shook. Snot poured from her nose and I wiped it away with an old handkerchief bearing my father's initials.

"I could use a dip," she said. "I'm pretty gross."

The pool was packed, the drained heat of a June day and a northern breeze conspiring perfectly. In the water we got into a splash fight with some kids, who retreated after absorbing a few of Molly's waves. Then we lay down in the grass, Molly gloriously supine, her thighs littered with freckles, necessary Norberg up on his elbows making sure the lifeguards didn't look too close. We strolled side by side on the path that outlined the fountains and ended at the pavilion.

"What do they understand about opera in New York anyway?" I asked.

"A lot, actually," Molly said.

"Opera is about failure and heartbreak. Near misses, tragically missed opportunities yearning, and nostalgia. Is there any better place to cultivate these feelings than in Trude?"

"Nice try, Norberg."

"Can the humiliation of *Pagliacci* really be understood by Wall Street bankers in several-thousand-dollar suits? Can the madness of Lucia be properly understood amid so many *fully occupied buildings?*"

"This is a great effort."

"Trude is opera," I said. "They should be coming here to study opera."

"What if they just measure things differently?" she asked. "When people in Trude say my voice is beautiful, is it just because they don't know better?"

I was unsure how to reply. The more I said, the more likely it seemed that I would confess to praying for this very outcome. From the very first mention of New York I had been terrified. Had I wanted her to fail? Because if those figures in the auditorium had taken her, it would have been one more piece of writing on the wall, foretelling the ways that I would eventually lose her completely.

We drank white wine and spread melted Brie over a baguette that we tore with our hands. As the sun lowered and blushed over the composers' sculpted heads, we felt, and our fellow Trudians must have felt, that there was nothing wrong with this place, that things could have been a lot worse. Schubert's Death and the Maiden was the centerpiece of the concert that night, and it was sometime during the slow buildup of the rondo that I slid my hand into Molly's suit and touched her with two fingers. She still smelled of chlorine. I moved my fingers in time with the music and Molly bit her lip.

"What do you think you're doing, mister," she gasped.

I wanted to be inside her. The way I wanted Molly made my desire for other women seem trivial, merely mechanical. When she pushed my hand away it felt like a mild amputation.

I CONCLUDED THAT it might be better to make an early exit. I had long lost track of Mozart, and my legs were puffy with mosquito bites. My shirtless neighbor watched me go, chip suspended on his lips, a look of rebuke almost visible behind his sunglasses. On my way out I passed faces that were darkened and critical, not much different, I thought, from the faces of the auditioneers who had waited below while Molly sang onstage, and who had called out abruptly "that's enough." We had left the pavilion early that night as well. The quartet was only halfway through the fourth movement of Death and the Maiden when the skies opened, going from zero to sixty as a Midwestern thunderstorm can. People who only moments before had been stretching comfortably and feeling relatively blessed now ran for cover and their cars. Having walked, Molly and I were stranded, but we also had our swimsuits, so we surrendered to the rain. I kissed her on the mouth. The quartet lingered faintly in the distance.

The white shirts of the musicians were like sails in the churning storm, which pushed napkins, wrappers, and takeout menus through the air. The trash caught on the composers' busts. In the distance the facades of the old fairground buildings swayed in the wind, their bricks nacreous with rain. Gray waves sloshed over the pool's rim. The thunder's symphonic bombast drowned out the quartet, and higher up the hillside, lightning struck a hubristic church spire. This was a storm to please even the most opium-addled romantic, and I took my cue, escorting Molly into the foliage of a stout oak. We were not the first to discover this bower; the tree's trunk was scarred with the initials of our predecessors. I could have carved *M + S* there but I had no implement, only my hands, pruny from the weather.

Molly was pressed against the bark, flushed and breathing hard from the run. Her eyes glowed, bright and alien. I reached for her slick thighs and lifted her. She always felt light to me.

"Listen," I said. "If I don't tell you this now, I'll never say it."

"You can say whatever you want." She smiled. "It's just you and me here."

Her red hair blazed against the dark green leaves.

"When you were gone," I said, "I was like a tourist in a strange city. No map, no itinerary, no landmarks. I was a guy with a camera around his neck strolling around in bad shorts."

She looked at me affectionately from the heights, like a teacher amused by an improbable excuse. "And I'm your map?" she asked. "You'll fold me in your pocket?"

"No," I said. "You're my reason."

"Well we wouldn't want you to go *mad*," she said before I stopped her short with a kiss, my lips coming away wet. I held her there against the crude and malapropic slogans of eternal love and asked my question. Could she feel them, the shape of the names, the curved humps of a heart, digging into her back? I wanted my words to be as tactile as those inscriptions. Water dripped from the leaves or her eyes.

"And if I say yes you'll let me down," she said.

"Probably." I laughed.

She descended, her lips brushing my ear as she whispered, and when I heard the sound I'd dreamed her saying, the one syllable with its sibilant end, I collapsed in bliss, landing in the mud beneath my shrieking fiancée. The happiest moment of my life took place in a puddle. I hadn't even brought a ring, but in Molly's presence I felt forgiven. She could make me forget myself and where I was; she brought me my only feelings of ecstasy. Looking at her, I was no more aware of my murky bed than the background through the canopy: the distant facades, the pavilion, and the vacant stage.

7

THE TRAUMHAUS WAS HIGHLY SELECTIVE. ACCORDING TO A *Trumpet* survey, one out of three Trudians felt that they could benefit from a stay there, but the ratio of admission was much lower than that—a far cry from the somewhat sluttish admissions policy at Trude U. The whole process was shrouded in secrecy. There was no clear science to it. Sociopaths, schizophrenics, the baroquely mad, were not admitted. Adolescents were not admitted. Illiterates were not admitted. Religious fanatics were not admitted, unless they had personalized their delusions in some compelling way. The average old were not admitted. Contented people were generally not admitted, though there were some exceptions. Typically depressed middle-aged males were not admitted. My own application to the Traumhaus, honed in the wake of Molly's disappearance, had been classified in this last category. It still stung. I consoled myself by using my visiting privileges three times a week. The Traumhaus seemed to be the only place where I could find peace. In the autumn its birches turned yellow and burnt orange, complementing the dark green of the pines almost too well.

To the charge that it was an "elitist institution," the Traumhaus responded with tranquil silence. As the reflection of the building in its pond suggested a castle, an element of gentility clung to the place. Though I might feel privileged each time I passed through the double doors, there was a sense in which I remained excluded, unselected. Some who had been living at the Traumhaus for years continued to feel this way. My mother felt this way at times. This largely had to do with the presence of the so-called Pinkies, a select caste within Traumhaus culture. They were special beneficiaries of Bernhard's will. It was easy to recognize them by their distinctive shuffling step, their looks of devastation, and the pink bathrobes they wore at all times— markers of a twenty-four-hour suicide watch. These pampered disconsolates wore clear plastic slippers and received their break-fasts on silver trays. They occupied the best rooms, overlooking the pond: the Robert Walser Room, the Klaus Mann Chamber, and the Schreber Suite, where Bernhard had spent the last months of his life. Pinkies were a rare sighting in the Wittgen-stein Lounge or any of the other public areas. When they passed, slippers squeaking on the linoleum, the other residents went silent and gawked at these suffering virtuosos—increasing, one can only imagine, the burden of disappointment and loneliness that had made them Pinkies in the first place. I could only guess at this loneliness, its rarefied depths, but I assume it was the reason I finally met one of them.

My mother had just humbled me at Scrabble once again, and I was making my way from the lounge to the Staircase of Reflection. I was stopped on the landing by a whispered "pssst" from the doorway behind me. "Pssst, pssst, pssst," said the voice, and I turned to see a ragged shape of a man in the doorway. The gold plate on his door read THE ROBERT WALSER ROOM. A pink-robed arm flailed, gesturing me in. "Pssst, pssst," it said, and I ended my hesitation on the landing. As rumored, the room was spacious and bright, with a comfortable-looking gray loveseat, a brown leather recliner, and a walnut desk which hoisted a manual typewriter and a tall stack of manuscript paper. French doors led to the balcony overlooking the pond. Sunset was maudlin: rays of blood orange and purple tinged the water and the wooden ducks.

My host closed the door behind us, knelt and pressed his eye to the knobless hole. "This is strictly against regulations, you understand, so stay quiet," he said. With his permanent hunch, swooping gestures, and pink plumage, he looked like an aged but defiant bird of prey.

"I am Vollstrom." He pointed to the white *V* embroidered on the breast pocket of his robe.

"Norberg," I said. "My mother lives in the . . ."

"Of course. A beauty, your mother, if you don't mind me saying so. God knows why she is fraternizing with that asinine old poseur, Harris."

"I agree."

"Give me your cigarettes," Vollstrom said, extending an unsteady hand.

After taking one for myself, I handed him the pack.

"How am I supposed to work if they keep taking my cigarettes?"

The room appealed to me. It had a clarity and brightness. Objects were sharp and distinct, and appeared to be lit from within. Sitting at the walnut desk, in the silence and sunlight, drinking French press coffee brewed by an attractive hausfrau, I might finally be able to sort through the unraveled text of my life and give it shape.

"You have a beautiful view," I said.

He laughed bitterly. "That is what they say! But you only repeat that trite observation because you did not see what happened to the ducks. Pssst," he said, waving his unlit cigarette. I handed him my matches.

"But the ducks are—"

"Fake? They haven't *always* been fake." Vollstrom raised a trembling flame, his drawn cheeks becoming skull-like as he sucked. His gray hair had congealed into a greasy hook across his temple. He shuffled to the window, his robe fluttering around his spindly, bruised legs. Long hooked toenails showed through his transparent slippers. "When I passed the tests and was admitted here," he said, flashing a yellow smile of accomplishment, "there were twelve ducks on the pond. Real ducks, mallards, not the *wood ducks* you see now. A male, a female, and ten chicks. Fluffy yellow chicks, the kind you might find in a sentimental painting at Bernhard's mall. They rode on their mother's back quite charmingly. I can still hear them peeping." He shuddered. "Out of sheer boredom—this place is detestably *boring*, above all—I used to count them as I ate my breakfast. One morning I noted that there were only nine chicks, that one of them was missing, as they say. I found myself intrigued by this mystery, if only because time passes so slowly here."

"You write," I said. "You have an excellent library."

"Yes, my child, but there was some *actual life* happening right outside this window." Vollstrom jammed his hands into his robe pockets. "I went to the balcony with my binoculars. To witness the magnified horror. The male duck plucked one of the chicks from the mother's feathers. He tipped back his head and broke the chick's neck with his beak, tossing the corpse into the water afterward. I watched him do the same to a second chick, then I had to look away. To think, the staff here tossed bread to that duck! They paid no attention to me and kept throwing bread in! Rewarding the murderer! The surface of the pond, which you call beautiful, was littered with bloody fluff."

Vollstrom stood at the window, appearing as a wobbly shade in the reflected castle down below. "The event was even more gruesome with my eyes closed, in the theater of my imagination. But that wasn't even the worst of it. After the ducklings were gone, *the very next day*, I looked up from my breakfast to see their wooden replacements. I knew then that Bernhard, that cold genius, had anticipated the entire scenario. He had sanctioned the killing of the innocent ducklings and arranged for the manufacture of their wooden replacements. All so that I would be reminded of it always, so that I could never forget."

I had to interrupt my lecturer. "Bernhard has been dead since 1983."

"In a way, that is true." Smoking incessantly, Vollstrom claimed that there was a basement in the Traumhaus to which the residents had no access. It housed the architect's corpse, which was stored in a wide-berth coffin in a temperature-controlled room. (This was not the first time I'd heard the rumor that Bernhard was entombed in the asylum of his own design. Pinkie claims were dubious, but widely reported.) The corpse, according to Vollstrom, was re-embalmed twice a month by an admiring mortician and consulted on key decisions by the senior attendants. With the aid of a full spectrum lamp and dated shock therapy equipment, they had reanimated Bernhard as a part-time administrator. Low voltage shocks from dozens of electrodes, attached to Bernhard's slack facial muscles, could produce either a "positive" or a "negative" expression.

"So they can only ask him yes or no questions," Vollstrom said. "For example, 'Is Vollstrom's memoir harrowing enough to admit him to the Klaus Mann Chamber?' Then they shock the corpse, and they interpret the face. The thing is, it's all so subjective."

Vollstrom circled the room, as if homing in on his precise grievance. "The most recent installment of my memoir was returned with the phrase 'insufficiently harrowing' stamped all over it. Can you imagine how it felt? How discouraged I became?"

"I'd like to read your memoir," I said.

"You'll find it in the library," said Vollstrom. "With all the others. It's part of the treatment. They are deposited twice a month, shelved side by side, and they molder away. Much as I have moldered away in the Traumhaus for more than two decades now. My memoir grows like some malignancy, feeding on itself. It has reached monstrous proportions. In order to really read me," he smiled impishly, "you too would have to be a resident here."

8

WHEN I FIRST MET MOLLY, SHE WAS WEARING A RED SWEAT-
suit and a gray plastic fish head. The annual Heaven/Hell
Halloween party took place in a dilapidated, beery Victorian at the campus edge. A wrecked Buick had been over-
turned in the driveway and stuffed with ketchup-stained
mannequin limbs. Upstairs, angels, fairy princesses, and a few
stray demons listened to Purcell and smoked pot; downstairs,
priests mingled with strippers and sociopaths under strobe
light. I stood in purgatory on the landing and smoked a cigarette. I was enjoying myself. Costume parties were the only
parties I'd ever enjoyed.

"What *are* you?" asked the fish in the red sweatsuit,
approaching.

"I'm the dictionary," I said, crinkling as I made room for
her. I reeked of glue. "And you're a red herring?"

"Nobody's getting it, plus I can't breathe," she said, in her
deep, almost masculine voice, and sat down next to me on the
landing. The red sweatsuit was refreshingly modest, I thought.

She was one of the few women in the house who hadn't taken the excuse to dig out fishnets, stilettos, and a black bustier. It was a two person job, removing the thick plastic fish head. When we'd finally twisted it off, I blushed, recognizing Molly. At that time in my life there was a certain kind of woman who made me want to fall to my knees and confess the wretchedness of my being. She was in the music school, an ivied enclave set slightly above and apart from the rest of Trude U, but she had descended to take up a chair in the advanced course Dead Ends of the Romantic Poets.

"Thanks," she said, looking me over anew now that she was out of the fish-eye. "So are you being consulted much tonight?"

"Sorry?" I was still trying to comprehend this sudden, dreamlike surge of good fortune.

"Are a lot of people looking for meanings in you?" Molly looked at me intently. Her watery green eyes seemed to absorb everything, from the print on my pages to the gestures and flirtations going on all around us, the tags in people's costumes, the scratches on the floor.

"Not really," I admitted. "Everyone's playing fast and loose with the English language tonight." I rearranged the red board on my chest that read, DICTIONARY OF THE ENGLISH LANGUAGE: SECOND COLLEGIATE EDITION. The words didn't exactly fall from my mouth with a burnished epigrammatic gleam.

Molly did not respond. "You're afraid of me, aren't you," she said. "You think I'm a lesbian."

"You're not?"

She shrugged, scanning the room and its scores of French maids, call girls, dominatrices. "Not exactly." She paused. "I was wondering what the third edition of the dictionary might look like."

I told her my plans. We were seniors and I hoped, more than anything, that I might find some way to delay graduation and postpone reentry to the so-called real world. "I'm thinking of studying law," I said. "I'm interested in divorce." My own parents had recently finalized their divorce, and I'd tried to nurture this easily foreseen event into trauma. Molly never forgot this statement or stopped mocking me for it. She would even introduce me, much later, as "my husband, who is interested in divorce."

I descended into Hell and brought back cheap beer in plastic cups. We talked and drank; as the conversation went on, my pretentions peeled away, and I found that I could talk to her in earnest. I remember the precise care with which I chose each word, glancing from my dictionary pages to the intricate pallor of her face. The amputated fish head watched us with dismay. Scantily clad partygoers passed us on their way to the bedrooms, clutching the banister. Two guys in ghost outfits hurtled around the house, crying "ooh-ie!" and pumping their fists out from their midsections. "We're masturbating ghosts!" they cried, and these two baggy forms cling like faded barnacles to the memory.

OVER THE YEARS I watched her die hundreds of times onstage. Being a mezzo, Molly was not typically given the grand fall of the soprano—she would more often be the loyal nurse who stumbled in and wailed, pulling at her hair. Still, when given the chance, as she was in *Carmen*'s climactic bullring many times, her deaths convinced. She took Jose's fatal knife in her belly, held it there for a few moments with almost maternal gentleness, then tumbled to her knees and collapsed to the floor with an inspired, bullish snort. In her villainous roles, too, she had ample opportunity to perfect her form. In Humperdinck's *Hänsel und Gretel*, she played the witch, heading for the oven with a final searing cackle. Watching these acts was a kind of inoculation. No matter how gruesome her demise, it would only be a few minutes before she would return to the bravos of the standing crowd. The flowers rained down on her but they were not funereal flowers, they were Easter flowers. She had come back from the dead. Maybe it was this simulation, so oddly calming, that made her loss impossible for me to conceive. Four months had passed since her disappearance, and I was still on my feet, clapping and calling "bravo." Only I was now alone in the auditorium, the curtain had closed, and the stage crew had long since gone home, switching the lights off behind them—I alone waited for her encore.

Her last interview had been granted, four days before her disappearance, to Martin Breeze. It would be too easy to say that he was a windy man, though he did wear loose berets and scarves, ruffled shirts that billowed. He had the cloudy, hopeful gaze of a man who'd lost the plot. His cummerbunds were crooked. He was pigeon-toed. His comb-over concealed a swelled skull. Still, it was Breeze who had blown the air into my wife's reputation and made her seem *larger than life*, and she'd reminded me to be civil to him before our outings to premieres at the Opera House. At after parties we would stand near each other, as Molly fluttered masterfully from group to group, chewing hors d'oeuvres over our little plates as I listened to the first draft of Breeze's columns.

BREEZE: You are now not only the preeminent mezzo, but arguably the preeminent opera singer in Trude.

NORBERG: But I'm getting old. [*Laughs.*] I'll give up some of the limelight to younger performers. I think people are ready for new faces.

BREEZE: I could not disagree with you more.

NORBERG: As you know, the repertoire for us [mezzo-sopranos] is limited. There are only so many nurses and witches you can do. You've sung Carmen a hundred times, you've sung Rosina. There are limits for a woman with a certain voice range. Once you reach that point, you can either rest on your laurels or go in a different direction. I don't want to be singing Carmen when I'm fifty and three hundred pounds. [*Laughs.*]

BREEZE: That is hard to imagine. To change the subject, you have developed a certain cult following here in Trude. Is it strange to run into your admirers?

NORBERG: I am incredibly grateful that people like my voice. I've made a living doing the only thing I really love, and how many people can say that? It is strange sometimes, though. I have my days. Those days when you're sick of yourself and wish you were someone else.

I couldn't really understand why my wife would ever have wanted to be someone else. But I'd never had her gift for self-transformation. Her peculiar magic was transitive. Even at our closest, there was a part of me who remained her spectator. She could become other people—how it dazzled my watching self and held him in naive awe. On those evenings when it was just the two of us, she made a special Molly just for me. Sweatpants-clad with her makeup off and her hair in a bun, her lips around a milkshake straw or a furtive cigarette of mine. "They'll never recognize me," she said, because this version of Molly loved subterfuge as much as any hooky-playing high schooler, even if her fans always found her in the end, wherever we went: the grocery store, the hardware store, the pizza parlor with its dusty red lampshades. She waited for the blushing, inarticulate praise to tumble from their mouths, then reacted with a look of surprise and gratitude. Molly claimed to be a second-rate actress but she did that look quite well. The moment they left, she returned to my Molly-on-her-day-off, the part she played when she didn't have to play a part.

Despite the fact that it was Molly who took my crumpled phone number on Halloween and called me for a date, despite the word she'd whispered in my ear by the pavilion, it was difficult for me to maintain belief. I never quite understood what she saw in me. Even after Kyle was born, when she looked into my eyes and said, "I'm never going to leave you, Iceberg" (she called me that when my feet were cold), there was a part of me that refused to accept my good fortune and engaged in a slow, relentless program of sabotage. My love for her was a nervous worship. With her success, our marriage became porous. Every admirer, male or female, was a potential rival, and my fits of jealousy were constant, sickening. The lithe understudy, the muscled tenor. The millionaire, the visiting college poet, the endless ushers. I don't know how she endured it all. "What would it take to convince you, to make you believe?" she asked in arguments toward the end, and I suppose if I had been honest, there was no right answer. There had been moments, whole days and weeks, as when she sang the Alto Rhapsody in the cathedral—when everything aligned, a clear sky, the fresh air, the chrysanthemums, my wife's vocal cords thrumming at the center of a harmonious world. Now that she was gone, it was as if all the nights of doubt had been justified. It was the oblivious, contented days that I regretted. I relived them, over and over, as Molly had practiced especially difficult lines in scores, but while she eventually mastered them, I never did.

OUR LAST NIGHT together was an ordinary one in every way. Molly came home from the opera, bitching about Strauss. We ate a late, quiet dinner of chicken parmesan without Kyle, who had eaten on his own after driver's ed and had adjourned to his room, not to be disturbed. While I did the dishes, Molly went upstairs to change into a nightgown, a worn gray dowdy thing with a white collar. She came back down and settled into her favorite armchair with a carton of mint chip ice cream, a spoon, and the book she was reading. It was a warm night and we had the ceiling fan on in the family room; it ruffled the pages of Molly's book, a hardcover with yellowed paper and a dark dust jacket. (In the days after, I scoured the house for this book, but I couldn't find it.) She was absorbed in her reading, and as I smoked my last cigarette of the day on the couch she barely looked up from the text, though usually she would give me subtle disapproving looks when I smoked in the house. She took dainty bites of the ice cream, which soothed her throat. I stabbed out my cigarette in the ashtray and went over to her chair.

"So I'll see you tomorrow after rehearsal?" I asked.

"Mm-hmm," she said, without looking up. She dug into the ice cream and, still reading, extended the spoon to the area where my mouth might be. "You should have a bite of this, it's delicious," she said.

I was full, but I leaned over slightly and took the ice cream. I held it in my mouth for a moment and let it melt, my cold, sweet substitute for a goodnight kiss. Halfway up the stairs, I turned to see my wife observing me with a studious, neutral expression. It was the look she might have subjected me to when trying to decide if a piece of spinach was still stuck between my teeth.

"Good night, Molly," I said.

There was a barely audible pause, an eighth or quarter note rest that might have meant more to her musical ear than it did to mine. Then she replied, "Good night, Sven."

9

THE THIRTEENTH HOLE AT SHERWOOD FOREST COUNTRY Club, par four, opens to a lovely downhill view of the old Trude Fairgrounds. Men in sweater vests pause there, putters in hand, to consider the urban ruin they've left behind. The metallic struts of the grand arcades stand like dinosaur ribs over pools of shattered glass. Nearby, the unburied bucket seats of the half-submerged Ferris wheel turn in the wind. A huge marble arch serves as a gateway between two empty fields. These fairgrounds hosted the 1898 Quite Grand Exhibition of Manufactured Wonders and Medical Curiosities, the event that still must be considered the turning point for our city. The story of the fair forms a long set piece in the course Trude: Its Brief Glory, Tragic Fall, and Long Decline, required for all-sixth-graders in the Trude public school system. My own sixth-grade teacher was a thin woman called Miss Herring whose dark clothes accentuated her nearly chalk-white pallor. Her glasses, sadly out of fashion now, were an enormous face-sized contraption of thick glass and plastic: it was hard to believe that they

enhanced her vision. Miss Herring described Mayor Trudenhauser's publicity campaign and the long preparations of the fair
builders. She told us moving stories of clockmakers and artisans
who had brought their life's work to the arcades for display. The
great arch was erected, the fountain that would gush water in all
the colors of the rainbow, the set of commissioned sculptures
depicting the Ages of Man. Two hotels were built for the fair
and hopefully christened the President and the Ambassador.
Macrocephalic babies and two-headed frogs arrived from obscure corners of the Midwest and were later immortalized as
grainy murk in Miss Herring's slideshow. She showed us mar-
vels: corn cob churches and enormous pigs. We sat glued to our
chairs as she took a brief detour into meteorology, clapping two
chalkboard erasers together to evoke the collision of fronts that
week in 1898. The yellow dust settled on the studious heads in
the front row. Miss Herring's two day account of the fair, lasting
as long as the fair itself did, was a tour de force. She glossed the
mechanical failure of the streetcar system. She recounted the
collapse of the arcades, pummeled by hail and tornadic winds,
then concluded her presentation with washed-out film of the
devastated fairgrounds, which had been recorded on an obsolete
Edison cinematograph. As the film surveyed the broken glass
and scattered violin pieces, Miss Herring led us in a recitation
of Lermann's "Ode to Trude":

> *Oh placid city, your souvenirs*
> *Of weathered brick and broken stone*
> *Remind us of the rubble of the years*
> *And failure written in the bone*

We pledge to stay and make repairs
Until a million lights are on
Until our illness disappears
And all impediments are gone

The cross-eyed boy who sat to my left either had not memorized, or could not utter, these terrifying and oblique verses. Miss Herring pulled him aside and dismissed the rest of us. We applauded her wildly, and she responded with a single, modest bow, her left hand still clutched on the delinquent's shoulder. Feeling much older than our twelve years, we filed out of the sixth-grade classroom and into the falling leaves.

CADDYING FOR BOGGS at the country club was one of my more humbling duties. It was a duty I performed on foot, because Boggs was a purist who thought golf was exercise. This ethos was perhaps best appreciated in the abstract, not with Boggs's clubs on one shoulder and J. B. Aabner's clubs on the other. The three of us passed from the thirteenth hole to the fourteenth tee. The wrecked arcades were no more than a pleasant shimmer in the distance. The trunk of the Great Arch was a dark blur. Trailing slightly behind, with the two sets of clubs clanking in stereo, I noted the contrast between the two aging legal playboys. Aabner, wearing a loose Hawaiian shirt and sagging elastic-waisted khakis, looked swollen from decades of sensual indulgence, like a debauched aristocrat in an Edwardian woodcut. The meaty back of his neck cooked in the late September sun. Boggs, on the other hand, looked spry and elegant in his golf duds. His tailored tweed pants fit perfectly. He wore a thin buttercup-yellow vest over a light blue silk shirt. I'd often wondered what it felt like to wear Boggs's clothes, the warp and weft of such fine fabrics against the skin.

He rested his hand on Aabner's back, unfazed by the rivulet of sweat that had formed along Aabner's spine, staining the palm tree on his shirt.

"Got a little of the old habeas corpus last night," Aabner said.

"That right?" Boggs replied. He'd lately grown weary of Aabner's Latinate kissing and telling. Sometimes, when Aabner called the office to narrate a recent conquest, Boggs would actually inspect a client's file to divert himself. I also had difficulty enduring Aabner's boasts. I couldn't help imagining myself splayed on Aabner's desk, under Aabner, accordion files and memo pads cutting into my ass—as I bore the weight of Aabner.

"Took me about six months to persuade her," Aabner said, "but damn, let me tell you . . ."

"I can imagine it well," Boggs said. "The longer you have to wait, the better." Boggs winked at me as he reached over my right shoulder for his driver. The graze of his hand felt like a caress, sending a slight shiver down my spine.

"Heh heh," Aabner chuckled dutifully. He took a nervous glance at me. Aabner had added the second *a* to his name in 1986, after the firm of Abner, Abner, and Boggs dissolved. The rechristening had vaulted Aabner above his father in the Trude yellow pages, but after Boggs invested in the cable TV ads, the ordering became, as these fellows would say, moot.

Boggs was still smiling at me, polishing his driver with a rag. His charcoal hair fanned in the breeze.

"Well," Aabner continued, "at least he carries your clubs. And it must keep Sheila happy, you having a male secretary and all."

Boggs scoffed and took a couple practice swings. He failed gracefully at golf. Boggs was having an especially erratic day at the tee, so I wasn't surprised when his drive veered far right of the fairway, landing in a narrow swathe of trees, the paltry remnants of Sherwood's "forest."

Boggs turned to me and shrugged. We strolled down the hill in companionable silence, leaving Aabner and his clubs behind. Eventually we found an entrance to the stand of trees. Boggs stepped gingerly to avoid soiling his polished brown golf shoes. Once inside, we were shielded from the golf course by leafy boughs and shrubbery.

He smiled wryly. "Here we are, Norberg, in a bower."

"I wouldn't call it a bower," I said.

"Is that so? What would you call it?"

I leaned his clubs against a tree and began poking through the undergrowth. "A wood, I suppose. A small wood."

"Here we are, alone together in the small wood," said Boggs.

I glanced at my employer, who stood smiling impassively under a weathered elm. Had he wooed my predecessors with such clumsy and unctuous endearments? The ancient love notes, many of them signed by "Willie," kept turning up in the corners of my desk and amid the files. They were addressed to Bridget, Jessica, Naomi, Annabelle, in the same looping cursive. My hire was meant to inaugurate a new marital and clerical regime.

I was determined to find his ball, suddenly. I sidestepped logs, pawed through fallen leaves. I beat back branches with his nine iron. Boggs, bemused, lingered on the edge of the wood, watching me work. What else was new. His ball was bright green, with BOGGS embossed on it in black. It was on the other side of a fallen birch, the bark fanning from the trunk like the pages of a waterlogged book. Behind the fallen birch was a small clearing, an inner enclosure. I stepped over the tree and reached for the ball, then recoiled when I saw a brown hand near it.

"Sir," I called, "we have a problem."

The man lay supine on a small circle of grass, marked by streaks of Sherwoodian light that slipped through the pines and birches. He wore a filthy blazer with holes in the elbows, a blue work shirt, and baggy pants with paint and turf stains. He was still breathing. Chunks of food were lodged in his long graying beard. He reminded me, oddly, of the man in my mother's story, the vagrant who had allegedly barged in off the street and disrupted my baptism. The impact of the ball had left a small cluster of red circles along his right temple, along with the reverse imprint of Boggs's name just above his eyebrow. I'd argued against getting the golf balls personalized, not that anyone remembered that now. The imprint would be enough to get this fellow a hefty settlement, assuming he could find his way to an attorney in time.

Boggs took a while to reach us. Stepping into the inner sanctum, he harassed a little tear in his tweed pants. "Oh my," he said, looking down at the man he'd felled.

"He's only unconscious," I said.

"Why don't you search him, Norberg."

I rifled through the man's coat pockets as he began to stir and groan, uncovering receipts for very small sums, wadded tissue, cough drop wrappers, a wrinkled letter written in Spanish, gum foil, and lint. Further investigations of the blazer uncovered (to my amazement) several completed crossword puzzles from the *Trumpet*. These crosswords, concocted by a reclusive puzzle genius fond of misdirection and self-quotation, were notorious for their difficulty and always stymied me. Yet the stranger had penned in a half-dozen of them, hardly striking a word.

"What about his pants?" Boggs asked from the edge of the wood, scanning the fairway for approaching golfers. He was ready to run at a moment's notice.

I turned the man over, reached into his frayed pants pockets, and found an expired library card with his name.

"Hey," I said, "I've read this guy's confession."

Boggs was nonplussed. I grabbed Jimenez and shook him hard by the lapels. Something tore. The detectives' exegesis had not impressed me that much, but still, it was cathartic to have a possible villain in my arms. "You hear me?" I said, slapping him in the face. "That's right, I've read your confession."

"Where am I?" Jimenez asked, opening his green eyes.

"Where is Molly?"

"I'm sorry, sir." Jimenez's beard bristled. "Do I know you?"

"You might know my wife," I said. "M-O-L-L-Y. Do those letters mean anything to you? Don't fuck with me now—I know how much you like *word games*."

He paused, cogitating, and rubbed his wound. "Good God," he said, "you're that poor man who lost his wife."

The perfect English this Jimenez spoke was a far cry from the colorful malapropisms of the confession, I realized.

"You must believe me," he continued. "I was not the author of that confession. All I know about your wife is that her recording of *Fidelio* is exquisite."

I softened. "If you didn't write it, who did?"

"The confession was the joint brainchild of McCready and his assistant, I'm afraid." Jimenez spoke staring straight up into the trees. His sentences were like the sunbeams that filtered through the interior—straight, long, luminous. "Your wife's celebrity has made this case a priority, and they've resorted to some dubious methods. McCready fancies himself to be a writer now, you know, and enjoys 'doing voices.' From the holding cell I could hear him reading passages to the Oracle, 'I wanted to cry like the females on this program' and so on. They were laughing hysterically. The code was the Oracle's idea."

In the distance, Boggs was impatiently hacking papery bark off a birch tree with his five iron.

"The Oracle forced me to sign the 'confession,' then released me, knowing he could never get a conviction. I am simply a public library patron who has nowhere to go since the crisis. I wander from place to place, thinking of the things I never had a chance to borrow. I am sorry about your wife. Furthermore, I am sorry for my involvement in that cruel joke."

"You okay?" I asked. "You need some ice or anything?"

"No, thank you," he said. "I am going to rest a while here, and then find someplace more secluded."

I left Jimenez in the bower with my number, which I'd scribbled on the back of Boggs's business card. On my way out I collected my employer's ball.

"Well done, Norberg," Boggs whispered in my ear, then cried "Here it is!" for the benefit of the distant Aabner who lounged, sunburned, on the green.

He didn't even take a penalty.

10

IT WAS IN OCTOBER, I BELIEVE, THAT I FOUND MY SON kneeling.

The house had settled into a disorderly decline, opening itself to molds and dusts that Molly had turned away. My weekly vacuuming sessions were nostalgic more than anything, a nod to tradition. There were still places I couldn't go, corners I left untended. With our clunky antique vacuum in tow I went downstairs, trying to make enough noise to warn Kyle of my approach. The basement was dimly lit and smelled of vanilla candles and patchouli incense. The scents of his nightly vigil could have covered the smell of pot, but they seemed more theatrical than pragmatic, an attempt to enshroud his activities with a solemn, ritualistic air.

He was kneeling by the bed in his boxer shorts. A glossy page was open on the wrinkled mass of the comforter. Kyle was murmuring something and moving his hands.

"Whoa, sorry, son," I said, abandoning the vacuum and beating a quick retreat to the neutral territory of the kitchen.

Halfway up the stairs I was already regretting my reaction. That "whoa" had been especially unfortunate. I could have done the adult thing and gone back downstairs to explain things right then, but I couldn't quite find the words. I stayed upstairs and after midnight I pulled out *Indecent Reference* from its stashing place under the sofa.

The next evening, after the hot dogs and chips were cleared away, I prepared the living room for a mellow but significant father-to-son conversation. The living room couch, where Molly had stretched her full length against the cushions, sipping wine, was one of the haunted heirlooms we skirted past. Her reading lamp was a complex, many-bulbed affair, an electrified bouquet, and I spent a lot of time twisting its metallic stems into a non-interrogatory arrangement. I tucked my shirt into my cords. Knocked on the door to the basement, as I should have the night before, and called for Kyle. He took the stairs in three giant strides and crossed the living room, flopping on Molly's couch. The leather huffed and squeaked beneath him.

I took a seat on the weathered armchair reluctantly. The twisted lamp burned between us.

"So what is it, Dad?"

Kyle sprawled back on the couch, his left foot dangling off it and grazing the area rug. The stiffness of the old armchair forced me to adopt a prim, upright posture.

"I wanted to apologize for last night," I said.

"For what?" Kyle asked.

I had worked out a short speech during the work day, even drawing on Boggs's mastery of all things carnal. (Not that he'd been much help: he had never spoken to his daughters about sex, he claimed, adding that their grasp of the subject was "intuitive.") Generously, I took all the blame for the awkward encounter the night before, vowing to better respect his privacy in the future. I told him that he had found a healthy outlet for his desires, that there was no need to conceal these activities from me. Being the elder male, I understood perfectly well how one's thoughts, when not otherwise occupied, tended to default to images of naked women in sexual positions, and that his activity of the night before might be considered a beneficial part of a full, satisfying existence in which one was a respectful friend to women. I had further thoughts on the subject but I could no longer ignore Kyle's recoiling. Far from being put at ease by my permissiveness, he had contracted to a tight ball at the end of the couch, knees wrapped in his arms. His cheeks reddened as he studied the ceiling. It was an inverted topography of textured drywall, rough as his face. I had often imagined myself walking weightlessly through the craters and gulfs of that upside-down landscape. My monologue had developed its own momentum, weirdly stronger now that I realized its effect on Kyle, and I kept talking until he interrupted.

"Dad, please," he said at last. "I wasn't doing that."

"But I saw—"

"That wasn't what you saw." He clutched his forehead, exasperated. "I wasn't doing it. But I know all about it from my sex ed class, so you're covered."

"It's okay, it's natural."

"It's lust." He implored the ceiling. "It's lust, Dad."

"I should have knocked," I said, retreating. "I was just trying to clean."

"*Dad*," Kyle said, leaning into the blinding light of Molly's lamp. "That was your illustrated bible I was looking at. I was *praying*."

THE GRAY VAN first trespassed onto the property just as I'd settled into my chair with the Sunday paper. It wobbled into the cul-de-sac slowly and uncertainly, and I took it at first for the vehicle of a confused plumber or electrician who would soon realize the mistake and retreat. But the van pushed forward into our uphill driveway and idled there for a few moments before sounding its horn twice. It was windowless on the sides and offered only dim glimpses of its driver and passenger: a man with a puffy beard and hair tucked into a chauffeur's plaid cap, and the thin, coifed blonde beside him. Obfuscated by the windshield, they looked like peripheral figures in a fresco. The van looked like a kidnapper van, it occurs to me now, though I didn't see it that way at the time, because the words FIRST CHURCH OF THE DIVINE PURPOSE were painted in bright yellow along its side. Apart from the bright yellow cross and the name of the church painted over the rear sliding door, there was nothing to distinguish the F.C.O.D.P. van from those traditionally deployed by so-called pedophiles, captors of helpless kids, who relied on windowless vans to shield their quarry from parental view.

I watched the scene as if it was just one more atrocity from the paper I was reading, unfolding far outside of my control. I listened to the front door open and close and watched Kyle descend the front stairs, walk down the drive, and climb through the sliding door, which opened automatically. He had combed his hair, wore a pressed blue shirt I didn't recognize, and held my father's illustrated bible under his arm. That bible had loomed untouched on the high bookshelves of my childhood. I had never seen the threat in it, never found the conviction to donate it or throw it out. The opening and closing of the van door garbled the church's name, as if it had been translated into a foreign language of which I did not speak a word. It was only when the van was pulling away that I began to grasp the signif- icance of what had happened. I was possessed by the strong feel- ing that at the very moment I most needed to intervene, I had done nothing. The gray van circled the cul-de-sac and made its puttering progress down the block, leaving a flourish of exhaust. Some minutes later, forcing myself upright, I went to the kitchen for a refill and found my son's simple note: *went to church.*

AFTER THE VAN'S growl receded, I returned to the paper hoping to find something to distract myself. Despite drinking half a carafe of coffee and smoking three cigarettes, though, I couldn't absorb more than a line or two of a story before irritably flip- ping the page. I remembered that Molly had wanted me to get my eyes checked. Unless I held it very close to my face, the type was indistinct to me. True, the *Trumpet* was infamously stingy with column space and ink. It was an inferior product for an inferior city, and as much as we complained, we secretly knew we deserved it. What's more, the *Trumpet* usually landed in the yard mangled, damp, or both, thanks to the bad throws of the third-rate paperboy. That Sunday the paper was badly damaged, A-1 through A-23 forming a waterlogged pastry of print. So I turned to the Leisure section. After its initial run on the front pages, Molly's case had been demoted to this home of specula- tion and gossip. It was tucked deep within the paper and its irrelevance had kept it dry. It was here in Leisure's journalistic backwaters that Martin Breeze was printed, his opinions as ephemeral as the scrawl a fishing line left in water. Breeze had made his living nibbling at my wife's talent. Since her disappearance I had deliberately avoided his column, The Opera Scene. But as it was Sunday morning and I was not a church-goer, and the rest of the paper was wet, I found my eye drifting back to Breeze.

His column was devoted to the Lyric Opera's new production of *Carmen*, which had premiered the previous Friday. The title role was, of course, supposed to be sung by my wife, who had already performed the part three times in extended and successful runs. In her absence, the role of Carmen fell to Ariel Perloff, who'd spent the last four years in Molly's long shadow as her understudy. Her image, sheathed in suggestive red roses, appeared everywhere now: on billboards, on the sides of buses, on fliers that fluttered past blighted buildings to land at my feet. Martin Breeze's column left no doubt where his sympathies lay—it was a ruthless performance even for him.

NEW *CARMEN* A DISASTER

Much has already been written about the long-awaited debut of Ariel Perloff in the Lyric Opera's production of *Carmen*. Languishing (justifiably) since 2005 as the understudy of much-loved mezzo Molly Norberg, who disappeared earlier this year, she finally had a chance to silence doubts and prove herself in the Opera House's spotlight Friday. However, her effort to sing perhaps the most coveted role in the mezzo repertoire was simply a disaster. Perloff's many problems began halfway into the first act. Her rendition of the Habanera was the most banal I've ever heard—wooden, often audibly flat, and worst of all, lacking even the slightest charm. It beggars belief that such a beloved role would be entrusted to this novice. Some may even suspect that Ms. Perloff did not so much earn this role as inherit it as the only daughter of iron-ore baron Paul Perloff and his new wife, Isabelle, the opera's powerful trustees. I don't advise going to this *Carmen*, this gawky insult to the future of opera in Trude. Despite the efforts of the director and supporting cast, this new Perloff production brings to mind the famous self-deprecation of Georges Bizet: "The people want their trash, now they have it."

Reading the damning words, I remembered Molly's impression of the young girl straining for a high note. Ariel had gotten on my wife's nerves, to say the least. She followed Molly from room to room in the Opera House and studied her every move. "Imagine being stalked by a twenty-two-year-old version of yourself, who is just as clueless and annoying as you were," Molly said once. I laughed to remember this statement but the laughter hurt my lungs. Breeze's evisceration had been enjoyable but the enjoyment didn't last, and I now felt more tired than anything. I returned to the bedroom to nap away the afternoon, but just as I was nodding off, the phone rang. Back in the old days, the calls had almost always been for Molly, and I'd let them go. But now I could never tell what news a call might bring.

"Sven Norberg?" asked a faintly accented voice on the other end.

I coughed in reply.

"This is Eduardo Jimenez." The caller seemed to be outside and using a bad public connection. "From the golf course," he said.

"Hello. How's your head?"

"The ringing has stopped. I sincerely apologize for disturbing you at home, by the way. I hope you weren't busy?"

"Me?" I looked around for an open pack of cigarettes and found one. "Where are you right now?" I asked.

"Um," Jimenez said, "I am not entirely sure. Either Sherwood Forest or New Arcadia, close to . . . the border? There is a large unmarked building behind me. The lot is full. People are emerging with laden shopping carts." There were sounds of freight trucks and approaching sirens. "Coupon day," Jimenez intoned solemnly. "In any case, I wanted to thank you for the consideration you showed me the other day, on the golf course."

"Happy to," I said. "I'm sorry that Boggs didn't apologize. He has a very limited sense of his own wrongdoing."

Jimenez spoke again but his words were swallowed by another belligerent voice. It was something about his avidity for crossword puzzles and how everything he read, at times, resembled an encrypted block that needed to be decoded. "So did you see it?" he asked.

"What now?"

"The acrostic in Martin Breeze's column?"

"The *acrostic*? Martin Breeze? Are you sure?"

Jimenez wasn't listening. I heard him trying to placate the foe who now seemed to be rattling or shaking something metallic. In a matter of seconds the phone cut off. I waited for a few minutes to see if he would call back, then figured Jimenez was out of quarters. Or maybe the pay phone had stopped functioning. The dead booths dotted the corners in Trude like empty confessionals. I went and found the paper where I'd left it, in a disheveled heap at the foot of my chair. I reopened the Leisure section to Breeze's column, which was directly across from the Sunday crossword, a time-consuming behemoth that must have taken Jimenez all morning. I reread Martin Breeze's column several times, first looking for a code similar to the one Mc-Cready and the Oracle had "discovered" in Jimenez's so-called confession. I then realized that I had overlooked a much more obvious acrostic:

NEW *CARMEN* A DISASTER

Much has already been written about the long-awaited debut
of Ariel Perloff in the Lyric Opera's production of *Carmen*.
Languishing (justifiably) since 2005 as the understudy of much-
loved mezzo Molly Norberg, who disappeared earlier this
year, she finally had a chance to silence doubts and prove herself
in the Opera House's spotlight Friday. However, her effort to
sing perhaps the most coveted role in the mezzo repertoire was
simply a disaster. Perloff's many problems began halfway into
the first act. Her rendition of the Habanera was the most banal
I've ever heard—wooden, often audibly flat, and worst of all,
lacking even the slightest charm. It beggars belief that such a be-
loved role would be entrusted to this novice. Some may even
suspect that Ms. Perloff did not so much earn this role as inherit
it as the only daughter of iron-ore baron Paul Perloff and his
new wife, Isabelle, the opera's powerful trustees. I don't advise
going to this *Carmen*, this gawky insult to the future of opera
in Trude. Despite the efforts of the director and supporting cast, this
new Perloff production brings to mind the famous self-deprecation of
Georges Bizet's: "The people want their trash, now they have it."

I felt a brief flash of pleasure, as if I had solved something or found a wad of money in the trash. Besides Molly's voice itself, this is what I had most wanted to hear. But my gratified faith, my forensic pleasure soon gave way to larger doubts. What do you mean, she is still singing? Where? To whom? And where would Martin Breeze, barely qualified to be an opera critic, obtain this insight anyway? Before long I had gotten dressed and was halfway downstairs before I realized that it was Sunday and that Breeze would be nowhere near his office at the *Trumpet*. My detective work, such as it was, would have to wait until morning.

THE *TRUMPET* BUILDING was one of the gorgeously encrusted brick buildings that lined old downtown. An ornate exterior frieze depicted Gutenberg perfecting his press, Luther translating the Bible into German, a medieval printer setting a block of type. Trude's early builders, those taciturn, credulous men, had known how to lay brick and cover it with carved stone. The building was half-empty now. The paper was abandoning the upper floors as circulation dwindled. I approached the front desk and a pink-nailed receptionist wearing a plaid skirt, belt, and pantyhose guided me toward an elevator with an old-fashioned brass grate. It was a creaky, uncertain ascent to the fourteenth floor. When I stepped off the elevator onto the worn carpet, I was relieved to see a band of light extending from Breeze's open door. I walked to the threshold and paused there. He had his leather jacket on and hunched close to a keyboard. Hearing my knock, he turned, the light from the dangling unsheathed bulb glinting off his round glasses. The rotation brought down his long gray fringe of hair. It was like a curtain he was constantly emerging from and retreating behind. He opened it with a casual flick of his hand.

"The ventilation in this place is wretched," Breeze said. "I'm trying to get a space heater up here. They tell me I might get the managing editor's. The old guy can't be trusted with a heater anymore—he leaned too close to it and his tweed coat caught on fire!" Breeze laughed nervously. "You should have seen him flapping around alight. I haven't run into you at the opera lately, Norberg."

"True. I hear Molly is still singing though."

"Hmm?" Breeze fumbled for a pencil and began chewing on it.

"I hear Molly is still singing." I passed Breeze a copy of his column, with the acrostic circled in red pen.

His hands trembled slightly as he inspected it. "Huh!" he said. He thought a moment. "You know, I have much less control over my column than you might think," he said. "When I was first hired here I had my youthful pretensions, but now I realize greater forces are at work. Take this building," he said. "Do you think it would be possible for a liberal paper to be housed in such a gloriously conservative building?" He pulled his collar up around his neck and shrank inside the leather jacket, looking pale and frosty in the blue light of his computer. "I am allowing larger forces to work through me. Anyone could do the job." He caught me with a significant eye before tossing back his hair. "Someone else with an average intelligence, vocabulary, and grasp of fundamental music theory and opera history could do the job equally well. You could do the job equally well, Norberg. That is what I realize now. I am a vassal. That is to say, a vessel. I am a body through which the language passes."

"So you had nothing to do with this acrostic."

"I wouldn't say that," Breeze said, reaching for one of the paper clips that filled his ashtray. It occurred to me that this was the first time I'd spoken to Breeze without a buffet between us. "You know me—I try to follow the plots. Sometimes it's not easy. Now, was the printed version of the Ariel Perloff article essentially my words, my thoughts? Yes. The gist was, Ariel Perloff is an embarrassment to our otherwise surprisingly decent opera company. Was the final column an exact, verbatim transcript of my words? I don't know. Let's face it, I'm not writing poetry here. Did I embed some sort of message about your wife in the article, which would rely on an exact knowledge of how the article would be typeset, not to mention a lot of inside knowledge about your wife, which nobody seems to have, not even the police?"

"So you're saying that the arts editor . . ."

"No," said Breeze. "I'm saying that I was a bit player in this. A cipher, a scribe, a channel for language at best. Do you really think that I'm the kind of guy to play all sorts of fancy word games?"

I sighed and sank back against the armchair cushions, which did not yield. "I had to read your column to find out what she was thinking."

"You mean that interview?" Breeze unbent a paper clip. "That was a full week before she unfortunately—"

"Yes," I said, "we weren't speaking all that much at the end."

11

WHILE KYLE SPENT HIS EVENINGS AT CHURCH, I WENT TO the mall. What odd peace I found there. Smoking in the parking lot's vast floodlit grid, I was supervised by the gray bulb of the water tower. At night the pace of commerce slowed and the halls were strangely hushed. Muzak played to a deserted food court. Tired retailers became sculptural and enigmatic in their chairs, languidly counting the day's take. I pressed past the kiosks and novelty stations and moved deeper in.

Perlmutter's Bookshop, stationed along an obscure curve of the mall's third ring, was not a thriving concern even in peak hours. Perlmutter himself had died six months before, leaving a legacy of customer complaints and unclassified volumes. The woman who'd taken it over had shoulder-length brown hair and wore cashmere sweaters and plaid skirts. Clara was her name, freshly printed on the plastic badge she wore around her neck.

The pleasure I took watching her struggle to organize the shop was hard to locate or justify. Lately I'd had plenty of time to contemplate how long it had been since I'd touched a woman's body, and in truth I was having a harder time enjoying my videos: I kept getting hung up on the fact that the belles of *Card Catalog Confidential* weren't real librarians. They probably weren't even readers, those lithe and tweed-skirted belles. Clara, by contrast, was the genuine article, a laid-off librarian forced by circumstance to confront Perlmutter's mostly used inventory. She worked in a systematic way, pulling and sorting from the beached boxes that lined the aisles, climbing stepladders to slot an orphaned title in, bending over the desk to check her bibliography on the computer. She had a peculiar sigh that started sharp, then slid down to cadence.

I grabbed a copy of Bernhard's memoir from the stack on the desk and brought it to the corner armchair. At this outpost I could read, or watch Clara, or gaze through the front windows at the consumers walking the hedge labyrinth, heads down. Toward closing time Clara would settle behind the desk herself, and the only sounds in the shop were our turning pages.

I only broke this silence once, to ask whether I was bothering her.

"I don't mind," she said. "I kind of enjoy having you there, like a gargoyle or something."

I smiled and returned to my reading.

MEMOIRS OF MY NERVOUS ILLNESS took its title from a book published in 1903 by Daniel Paul Schreber, a baroquely crazy Prussian judge who wrote a long, vivid, heavily footnoted book to establish his sanity and in the end proved just the opposite. Bernhard's memoir was published posthumously in 1984 and seemed to have been written with great reluctance. Feeling that his buildings were unappreciated, watching his "slum of a body" decay daily, Bernhard wrote his bitter book from the newly completed Traumhaus during one of Trude's coldest winters. "I spent my whole life waiting for a convalescence that never arrived," he wrote from the Schreber Suite. Bernhard had left Europe almost fifty years before. Disgusted by the athletic bodies on display at the 1936 Berlin Olympics, he fled to America, though he avoided the orange groves and beaches of Southern California favored by so many of his fellow émigrés, settling instead in Trude, "a city that was as sick as I was." Depression-era Trude was a truly bleak place, as the theatres and mansions of the 1890s had already fallen to ruin, without gaining the historic cachet they have today.

The young Bernhard found work at a brick-export business and lived in a squalid rooming house, where he worked on his English, lost his virginity to a toothless prostitute, and contemplated what he called "the Weimar solution." His despair lessened as his English improved, and he discovered the haven of the Central Library, chiseled with uplifting quotes and studded with churchlike stained glass windows. He studied European and American architecture at a long wooden desk every night until the library closed.

Bernhard's work as a brick exporter brought him into contact with buffs and preservationists, who often waited at the sites Bernhard was sent to, imploring his firm not to demolish the buildings it had cheaply bought. It saddened Bernhard to destroy an early movie house or a grand and decrepit hotel, but he saw his work as necessary violence. "I was a clearer of rubble, a germane destroyer of old forms," he writes, with characteristic wry hyperbole. He soon encountered architects as well. Horst von Hartsig, the well-known beaux arts architect and winner of the Prix de Rome, took special notice of the ambitious young man. He hired Bernhard as an assistant in 1942. "A useless person, who tacked a 'von' onto his name to impress naive Midwesterners," writes his former protégé. "Von Hartsig's false nobility did not enhance the quality of his buildings."

This may be a retrospective justification on Bernhard's part. Soon after accepting the job, Bernhard seduced von Hartsig's wife, Ulli, who remained Bernhard's great love until the end of his life. He even built an Ulli Room in the Traumhaus to memorialize her "gentle but genuine madness." Still in the "daze of Ulli," the young architect took the lead in several von Hartsig projects, including the restoration of the Opera House. While Bernhard found these projects disgustingly conventional, he gained practical experience, and fought his first battles with the infamous Trude zoning board. Von Hartsig continued to promote his assistant's career, which led to several commissions, mostly houses, in the late 1940s.

The great split between von Hartsig and Bernhard occurred in 1951. The two men stopped speaking for reasons that can be easily inferred. Bernhard left von Hartsig to start his own firm, and the two volleyed invective through the editorial pages of architectural journals for the next decade. To Bernhard's dismay, Ulli chose to stay with von Hartsig even after the revelation of her affair. After von Hartsig's death in 1964, she never remarried, dying herself soon after in 1968. Oddly, von Hartsig's will designated Bernhard as the architect of his tomb—either a final gesture of forgiveness or vanity winning out. Perhaps von Hartsig wanted more than anything to survive, if only as a footnote in his entomber's biography. After Ulli's death, her coffin was lowered into the adjoining plot.

Bernhard's grief, no doubt, contributed to the magisterial melancholy of his later work. The Ringstrasse Mall, "misunderstood by millions of corn eaters," was his great statement on the impossibility of fulfillment within a capitalist culture. It was very nearly never built. Fourteen years in the making, construction was delayed every step of the way, with Bernhard fighting heroically—others would say megalomaniacally—for the total realization of his vision. The mall was his *gesamtkunstwerk*, complete with outdoor leisure park, an amphitheater for classical music, latticed follies where serious young people could write novels, and a monorail line that would feed mallgoers to the downtown area and vice versa. Some of these features were sacrificed during the construction process, causing Bernhard to disown the project almost immediately after its completion. He reminded his partners that he (Bernhard) was the only one who knew the solution to the mall's central labyrinth, and would only reveal this secret when his specifications were met. They never were.

The Traumhaus was the consummation of Bernhard's late style. Funded by the wealthy heiress of a vacuum cleaner fortune, who gave Bernhard a blank check in exchange for a room in the finished asylum, Bernhard began work on his most personal project in 1977. He had been suffering from severe health problems for the past few years and realized he did not have long to live. Childhood memories came flooding back to him, inspiring the Alpine-style hiking paths and the artificial mountain he added to the wooded 120-acre lot. The plan for the Traumhaus was just as finical and exact as the one that had hampered the mall project, but in this case Bernhard was in almost complete control. The building's many eccentricities must be a result of this. Bernhard's instructions for day-to-day operations were followed religiously after his death, probably the origin of the Traumhaus myth that the architect was sustained on life support in the basement.

One of the Traumhaus's major innovations was the focus on writing. "In other words," writes Bernhard, "we wanted to reverse the usual relationship between memoir-writing and confinement. While Judge Schreber wrote with the hope that his massively insane book would convince the doctors to release him, we would like writing to be a means of admission. That is to say, writing as a way *in*. If your memoir is disturbing enough, we will open a room for you here, where you can live in your dream. As long as you continue to trouble us, you can live here in peace." Bernhard's memoir was the first to be submitted to the advisory board in the spring of 1980. A month later, Bernhard was admitted as the first patient to the home he had designed.

WE READ QUIETLY, and on those evenings my attention was divided between Bernhard's book and the woman I admired. It felt like a kind of mercy to have my attention divided in this way. The architect's voice on its own was too harsh—it needed to be diluted—so every few pages I looked up at Clara stroking her hair or plucking eyebrows that weren't orderly enough for her liking. When the phone rang, it was almost always a call for Sparkles, Cuz!, an immensely popular teen boutique whose phone number differed from the bookstore's by only one digit. Clara offered the correct number kindly, though a look of defeat sometimes crept over her as she hung up the phone and reached for the stereo dial to turn the music back up. Like me, she gravitated toward the songs and etudes of the melancholy and tubercular Schubert.

The shoppers passed by, sometimes two or three times because Bernhard's labyrinth had fooled them. They did not approach Perlmutter's dense shelves. They headed for the lingerie mannequins in shined windows, the balloons twisted into amusing shapes, the animatronic madame who told fortunes and took quarters. Clara watched them go with a sigh, glancing up from her flattened pulp novel.

In the absence of customers, it was possible to mistake the bookshop for a living room, a shared privacy, and the chamber music made me feel closer to Clara. This was what I missed most, the reliable physical presence of a woman who sometimes dipped a strand of hair in her tea by mistake, or let her fingers graze the mole on her neck, which was somewhere to the northwest of where Molly's had been. It was almost enough, when Clara's hair hung in her eyes, to pretend that I was at home reading with my wife. That Molly would look over at me and ask me how my day had been. But then Clara would move her hair, revealing the face of a stranger, and I was left with my usual hollowness and the guilty pleasure I found in her presence.

Regretfully, I reached the final page of Bernhard's memoir, a surprisingly tender passage in which he spoke of Ulli as "the missing heart" of his architecture. I closed the book, but I was out of sync with Clara, who still had a few pages left in her detective novel. I waited for her to finish, imagining her satisfaction when the villain was outed, then carried Bernhard's book up to the counter.

"You're a very careful customer," she said.

"I like the atmosphere," I said, almost adding "and the company."

"Thorough." She punched the total into the antique register, which slid out with a harsh chime. "Is there anything else I can do for you?"

I fingered the tattered dust jacket of the warped hardback. "No," I said. "Thank you."

The mall foyer was full of pale shoppers who clung to half-empty bags. I turned back to look at Clara through the glass; she rose from her desk, walked over to the armchair, and slotted her novel back in a gap in the mystery section, which had been obstructed by the head of her gargoyle. She gave no sign of missing him, me. My car was just outside, in the Mastodon lot, but at the last moment I opted instead for a calming detour in the maze Bernhard had built.

12

HALLOWEEN, I KNEW, WOULD NOT BE AN EASY HOLIDAY FOR me. Molly and I had always treated Halloween like Valentine's Day, leaving a bowl of candy on the step while we slipped away for a quiet dinner out, to commemorate our meeting on the steps between Heaven and Hell. That, of course, was not an option this year. I hunkered down in the house, lights off and shades down to evoke the dwelling of a misanthropic recluse. But neither these measures, nor the night's unseasonal humidity, prevented a parade of sweaty zombies, miserable robots, and gasping princesses from climbing the steps to collect stale jellybeans that I poured for them out of a misted bag. Mostly the black ones, which Molly had never liked.

I was sweating inside my mask. An impulse buy, charged to Boggs's credit card along with his condoms, it had cost $3.99. It had a half-stitched head wound and a long black mane that I stroked back with my clammy hand. I'd slit open the mouth so I could smoke and drink through the mask, and the two narrow eyeholes permitted a blinkered vantage on an old VHS tape of

Molly in Bartók's *Bluebeard's Castle*. She was standing under a doorway beside a crazed baritone in a flouncy robe.

Whether it was the eyeholes or the decayed quality of the VHS that made the spectacle appear as if it had been filmed from a gauzy distance, I can't say. Kyle had gone to an overnight lock-in at the church, which would insulate him from the pagan holiday and my dour company. It seemed that I had survived the worst of the night. Word had gotten out about the stale jelly-beans and traffic was slowing, leaving me to my solitary masque. When the doorbell rang around 10:30, I was prepared to empty the rest of my supply into the bags of the stragglers.

IF I DIDN'T recognize her at first, that was the fault of the peep-hole. It compressed figures into squat lumps. All night it had been doing the same thing to the kids. I saw a flattened beehive wig, a miniature lady pressed into evening wear, who appeared to be drowning in a puddle of hair.

It wasn't until she came inside that I saw Plea's swollen eyes, the frosting in her wig. She was wearing an elaborate white dress with an undercarriage, but it was deeply besmirched with chocolate frosting and cake crumbs. The more intact slabs of frosting showed fragments of an inscription. Her gray coiffure slumped to the side, revealing some of her actual hair, and a bloodied piercing in her left earlobe. The white fabric of her dress was sweat-soaked, showing through to what prudes of the past would quite rightly have called her unmentionables. The red guillotine line on her neck had blurred and smeared.

"I'm sorry," she said. "I didn't know where else to go."

"Plea . . . what happened to you?" I brought a roll of paper towels and started wiping the thick gummy cake from her shoulders and the back of her neck, coming away with heavy handfuls of it.

"They came out of nowhere. History repeating itself, I guess." She laughed, but this brought more tears and a gush of snot. "This is getting gross," she said. "And I was so stupid. I sold those cakes to them."

"Shh, shh."

She was tugging at her undercarriage and I helped lift her skirt. Imprecise with wine, I touched her body accidentally in a number of places. I wasn't disgusted by this contact, far from it. The warmth of her neck and back had passed into my hands. I retreated and set the undercarriage at the side of the entrance-way: it quivered there, a fragile and useless architecture.

"Listen," I said. "Why don't you go down to Kyle's room, take a shower if you want. I'll get you something to change into." I stopped, recognizing what this would entail. "And then I'll take you home," I added quickly.

She shook her head. "I can't go home. Nobody's there."

"Your parents . . ."

"Are at an all-night recreation of the masked ball from Schnitzler's *Traumnovelle*. Don't ask. I just don't want to be alone right now."

I considered the queen consort in her deflated dress. "You can't call?"

"No phones." She smiled ruefully. "It's a strict period thing."

I didn't say anything. Maybe I couldn't verbally assent to this situation, although it was already in motion, was already happening as I made to leave the room.

"Nice mask, by the way," Plea said.

Rain began to fall like a steady, incongruous round of applause. I climbed the stairs, passing my wife's faintly lit, painted image, her crowds of gray suitors. I tried to recall the name of the movie Molly told me the paintings reminded her of. Certainly she'd told me. It must have been one of those conversations during which I was only kind of half-listening to my wife, an attitude that shocked me now that it became less likely with each passing moment that I would ever hear her voice again. At the landing I stopped for breath, leaning my hand on the banister like an old man. I missed so much, I thought. Now I'm just a masturbating ghost. I glanced down at the TV where a tenor was stilled mid-aria, throat open, hand raised, squiggly pause line bisecting his belly.

I opened Molly's bedroom closet and inhaled its crypt-like odors. The gowns hung in a row, their rhinestones gleaming, an archive of gorgeous skins that had been shed. I parted the watery silk. None of this would do. What I wanted was her gray nightshirt with the white collar. That durable, unflattering garment was something I wanted to see worn again. I shoved and elbowed the gowns as I dug for the nightshirt, but it did not turn up on the hangers, in the hamper, or in the wardrobe. Which was odd, because Molly couldn't sleep without it. It will turn up, I thought, as I went downstairs with Molly's workout clothes, a pair of loose sweatpants and a T-shirt for a defunct punk band called THE ROTTING KISSES. I hoped they would fit. When I reached the living room I paused a moment to consult the tenor whose raised hand seemed to suggest that I stop right there, instead of descending to the basement. I dismissed him with a quick flick of the remote and went downstairs.

Kyle's room now resembled a spare subterranean cell. Most of his belongings were packed into a row of white garbage bags in the garage. Little remained: a few pens and notebook pages on his neat desk. The posters of hair rockers and cinema robots had come down, leaving a dim, tacky residue on the walls. The sole remaining image, more prominent for all the blankness that framed it, was a sleek and shirtless young man with long blond hair posed against an archery target. His arms were spread against the black and white rings, coolly daring the viewer to pierce his body with arrows or nails. Large crimson letters spelled out the name SEBASTIAN. A few feet under this poster, Plea was swaddled to the neck in Kyle's comforter. She flinched as I entered the room.

"Listen," she said. "We have a situation. We have a corset situation."

"Okay." I backed up the stairs.

"Which is that I may need help getting out of this thing. And I do need to get out of it. It's causing me intense pain. But the thought of being seen in it is also pretty painful."

"I doubt it looks *that* . . ."

"I don't know if you know how a corset works? Here's my honest assessment. I look like a girl with pretty nice boobs and a flat stomach, but there's like this loaf of unbaked bread dough around my midriff."

"Okay."

"I'm just verbally preparing you for what you're about to see."

"The corset needs to come off."

"It needs to come off, but there's something you could do that would reduce the um . . . mortification, for me."

"What's that?"

"If you took your clothes off as well, it would make things easier."

Staircases and landings are areas where I make poor decisions, I thought to myself on the stairs, as I removed my socks. Plea's idea was fair, but it was a bad idea in all other respects. I lifted my shirt, unbuckled my pants, and dropped the garments along the edges of the stairs, as if making way for an expected guest. If I'd been soberer I wouldn't have so quickly unsheathed a body that had been ravaged in recent months. My skin was pasty and pale, the coils of body hair shining with sweat. Plea would see it all, and no amount of quasi-paternal bluffing could conceal how I really felt about her.

She laughed when I returned to Kyle's room.

"That includes the mask, Norberg."

As I approached the bed, half-erect, I discarded the monster mask. I knew my hair would look bad after a night beneath it. She would see the bare patches of my scalp under the thinning strands. But she smiled at me. She moved the coverlet to the side, and there was nothing between me and her very wide eyes, which were full of apprehension. I also saw her breasts slumped on the ivory corset, her stomach, her blue panties and lightly stubbled legs. I was not ready for this new body. But the dissenting voice in my head faded as I approached.

We spoke in whispers. I told her that I was almost forty years old. It had been a while since I'd been close to anyone, and I was worried that I would disappoint her. Maybe this was a mistake. She pressed her finger to my lips. If I pretended she was beautiful for tonight, she said, she would forget about all that. This would be our secret. No one had to know.

I knelt over her and performed the ministrations of a lady-in-waiting, dextrous movements that required a concentrated gaze. She laughed as I undid the twined corset ribbons, loosened them from the eyelets. Her body relaxed and her organs returned to their natural alignment. With trembling hands I slid her panties down her thighs and over her ankles. In a spirit of solemnity I lowered my head and asked if she wanted me to stop.

She pressed my head between her legs and giggled as my tongue moved.

She grabbed my puzzled meat and asked if she grossed me out.

Our bodies lurched together. I licked the sweat from her shoulder, tasting sugar from the cake. She held my ass, guiding me deeper into a warm grip that felt too good. Her flesh rippled beneath me in pale waves. It was a factually beautiful sight but too intense. My eyes flickered to the periphery of this strange, bare room: Kyle's pens rattling in their mesh container, the eyes of the teen idol watching impassively from the wall. We were conspirators in the darkening room and I felt certain that someone had seen us, that this desperate act would soon be reported back to the actual world.

Halloween had ended. Our costumes lay in a jumbled pile. The rough stubble of her armpit provided cover for my tears. Residual shivers ran through my body while I wondered where my mask was. I reached for her small hand and gripped it hard, as if it was the only thing that kept me from drowning in the soft pool of my son's pillows and sheets.

I WOKE NEXT to a body-shaped imprint in Kyle's bed. Half-consciously I smoothed the sheets with an erasing hand. Last night's encounter had the blurry implausibility of a dream, and I waited to remember the falling plane or slanted building in which it had taken place. The fact remained, though, that I was in my son's bed for some reason—as Sebastian confirmed, smiling deviously from the wall. I turned among the unfamiliar pillows. My fluffy accomplices lay silent and inert, clinging to stray hairs of hers. Catching Plea's fragrance, an overpowering jasmine scent that must have come from the mall, I leapt out of bed, trailing the sheets behind me. Once I'd deposited them in the washer I returned for the under-sheet and pillowcases.

As I was disposing of this evidence, the doorbell rang, its call harsh and incongruous. I doused the sheets in detergent, unsure whether to answer. The second buzz doubled in duration. As the white cotton whirled in the dryer, I staggered into my crumpled clothes and up the stairs.

McCready and the Oracle bulged on the other side of the keyhole, their chubby faces solemn. The blue uniforms they wore seemed to signal some kind of demotion. "Good morning, Norberg, hope we didn't wake you," McCready said, pushing through the door the moment I unlocked it.

"No, I was just doing some laundry."

"It's not a crime." McCready winked. "You will remember my partner. Please forgive him—the Oracle has lost his voice."

"Don't be melodramatic," whispered the Oracle, leaning close enough to spit in McCready's ear. "It's only laryngitis."

I offered them coffee, which the Oracle ordered black, McCready with several spoonfuls of cream and sugar. My old-fashioned percolator shivered and sighed, its orgasmic-sounding exertions amusing to the former detectives, though not at all to

110

me. We gathered around the coffee table with our steaming mugs and lit cigarettes. McCready and the Oracle took the leather couch, while I sat in the big armchair. I left the lamp off, dreading its brightness. It was a drab, muted day, the gutters still discharging last night's rain.

"We apologize for just dropping in like this," McCready said. "The reason we came is that the Oracle had a dream last night."

The Oracle nodded and exhaled a comma of smoke. He reached into his pocket and produced a small journal with pastel constellations and iridescent moons. He found the most recent entry and handed the book to McCready.

McCready grinned wryly. "Yes, we know, Norberg, what could be duller than someone else's dream." He crossed his legs and pulled a pair of drugstore reading glasses from his shirt pocket. "But surely you will acknowledge that there are gifted people whose visions should be attended to in every detail. Not only that, but reread and reinterpreted, dwelled upon."

"It was about your wife," the Oracle croaked.

"I really think it's better if you don't talk," McCready said. He glanced at me over the rims of the glasses. "Norberg, you look uncomfortable. You're sweating and trembling. Is anything wrong?" I shook my head, willing my hands into quiescence. "It's not *that* kind of dream about your wife, don't worry. Though to be sure, many have had that dream." His gaze returned to the page. "Okay, here we are. The Oracle is taking your wife to some sort of clinic. Driving M. Norberg to clinic for a procedure, it says here. But we don't know what kind of procedure, right? The dream wasn't that specific?"

The Oracle shook his head.

111

"They used to be *very* specific," McCready said. "He dreamed that the First Bank of Trude was going to be robbed, and we were waiting there the next day when the prophesied getaway car arrived. He saw the make and the model and everything. In any case. *Clinic does not resemble usual medical clinic. Has two owls along front staircase, as at Central Library.* Hmm. That's interesting. A symbol of wisdom, of course. *M. Norberg is put under and carried upstairs on a gurney for her operation.* Very strange. *Meanwhile I sit in waiting room with thirteen women. They all wear glasses. They are all reading books in ancient languages of which I have no comprehension.* Hmm. Pretty weird, my friend."

The Oracle let his blond head fall back against the cushions. He looked weak, as if this retelling of his dream was draining him further.

"Coming to the end here," McCready said, flipping a page. He seemed to be editing out certain details he felt unimportant or inappropriate for my ears. "Ah, here we are. *After several hours, a doctor descends the stairs and tells me that M. Norberg's operation is complete. He asks me to come with him. He is very young and for some reason I do not believe he is a doctor. Nevertheless, I follow him up the stairs. The thirteen women look up from their books and watch us climb the stairs. We reach the landing and . . .* Here the dream ends abruptly."

McCready snapped the Oracle's dream journal shut. He leaned forward and slurped up the remainder of his cooling coffee. "Well, there you are, I guess. The Oracle's dreams should be contemplated for some time. He doesn't always immediately appreciate the full significance of them himself. I'll have a transcript sent your way."

While McCready excused himself to the restroom, the Oracle lifted himself off the couch. Ignoring me, he walked over to the stairwell and gazed up very intently, as if comparing these stairs with the ones he'd dreamed about. He started up, examining the series of paintings along the wall.

"Who is the painter?" he whispered.

"I don't know," I said. "An admirer of my wife's, I think."

"Interesting," he croaked. "The shadowy figure with the gray tie."

"Yeah—I could never figure out what he represented."

The Oracle turned and, leaning a hand on the banister, spoke almost inaudibly. "Perhaps it's you?" he asked.

THE OPHTHALMOLOGIST, WHEN I SAW HIM AT LAST, PRE-
scribed strong contact lenses. "I don't know how you even
function with vision like that," he said, fingering his pristine
white coat. I thanked him and told him I was hoping to read the
chalkboard, because I was going back to high school that night
for Kyle's parent-teacher conferences. It was one of the official
duties I could no longer avoid, formalities that hadn't simply disappeared with Molly. Her way of groaning through these events
had always made them more bearable. Humboldt High was a
squat, square brick building with long vertical slit windows that
made it look like a bunker or a top-secret government agency.
It was a good example of the paranoid architecture that had
thrived in Trude circa 1963. I parked the car in the huge lot and
joined the herd of parents.

The protocol at Humboldt, for its semiannual conferences, was to run the parents through a miniature version of the
child's school day. Upon my arrival a buttoned functionary
handed me a class schedule and a couple of Humboldt pencils,

then guided me down the hall toward Kyle's first-period class-room. The other parents seemed enthusiastic. Actually, now that I looked closer, there was something incongruous about their dress—so many leather jackets, hooded sweatshirts, and baseball caps. Had I missed something in the invitation? Pudgy middle managers adopted a foot-dragging lope. Stout suburban moms wore torn jeans. Everybody had pulled out their old sneakers and combat boots. Dressed in a button-down shirt and khakis, my Boggs office wear, I moved among them awkwardly as ever.

There was something strange about being at school at night. Moonlight brightened the edges of the goalposts on the football field. It was all ultra-crisp, almost too clear, through the new lenses. Kyle's teachers presented compressed synopses of their classes for our benefit. His Algebra II teacher turned out to be a bubble-gummy blonde, barely twenty-five, big silver hoop earrings and a provocative gray skirt. Her lip gloss glinting in the halo of the overhead projector, she parsed an equation under the wily gazes of aging dads. I kept to the corners, away from the pockets of gossip where rumors of my absent wife traveled from cupped hand to cupped hand. These were the same women who had approached Molly breathlessly in the hallways in past years, the same men who had winked at me from a respectful distance, as if to say "well done." This year silence and avoidance seemed to be the rule. It had been long enough that no one wanted to mention her above a whisper, all those whisperings creating a static around me, like the hiss of a record.

I arrived on time to Kyle's fifth-period class, Wood Shop, but I was one of the few. The instructor, a rough-hewn, sociopathic-looking fellow with hair growing out of his ears and undershirt, didn't help his own cause by scolding the latecomers and barking for quiet. The parents, forced to endure this so-called class for a full fifteen minutes, began to rebel. Small silver flasks traveled sub rosa and some of the parents were pretty soused, openly jeering the wood teacher's ruminations on logical construction and precise measurement. Somebody fired a spitball, high and off the mark. It caromed off a framed portrait of the wood teacher's two sons. It was a sobering moment, but it didn't last. Secrets were being shared in the ambient light of the slideshow. Marriages renewed themselves behind the lathes.

The teachers' presentations were followed by brief freeform periods, which gave the parents time to go out to their cars for a smoke or to refill their flasks. I asked a couple of the loitering teachers about Kyle. The algebra instructor's eyes glazed over—she resorted to negatives, noting that he had never disrupted her class, and that there were no major problems with his proofs. His health teacher, a wary-looking man with hollow eyes, mentioned that Kyle had "some very strong opinions about abstinence." I chuckled, shifting my weight inside my pants. After biology, in which the teacher felt compelled for some reason to defend Darwin's theories at length, looking directly at me, I slipped into an obscure bathroom for a cigarette. The tile pattern was an unlikely combination of burnt orange, turquoise, and charcoal gray. Behind one of the stall doors, also burnt orange, were a pair of black slipper shoes and sniffling and crinkling sounds. I got only two or three quiet drags in before my fellow fathers descended, demanding cigarettes. I fanned out the pack with a sigh. Most of them hadn't smoked in years. They coughed and fumbled with my lighter. Making conversation, I said that this parent-teacher conference seemed a lot different than the ones I'd attended in previous years.

"Well, yeah," said the man to my right, hairline receding, shirt artfully torn at the shoulder. "Didn't you read the letter?" He recited a few lines from memory. "Come as you were, before the kids, before the bills, before it all got real . . ."

"Exactly!" someone cried from the stall.

I had almost escaped when a throng of mothers entered the men's room, laughing dangerously. Soon I was bumming smokes to flirtatious matrons who wore their cardigans around their waists and puffed with flair. I decided to skip gym. My eyes had almost accustomed themselves to the absurd burnt-orange-turquoise-charcoal color scheme, and I wondered if this had been intentional on the part of the architect, a misguided sixties idealist summoning de Stijl. Had he considered that his wacky color scheme, after such a long exposure to it, would begin to seem bland and predictable?

I was on my way out again when a firm hand stopped my progress. "Hey, you're Sven Norberg," the woman said. "Honey, this is Sven Norberg," she said to a co-smoker across the room.

I couldn't deny it—it was on my nametag. The woman's nametag read PRISCILLA. There was a luminous darkness in her eyes, which she'd accentuated with eye shadow to match the inky streaks of dye in her hair. She had the golden chemical skin of a frequent tanner. The nails that gripped my shoulder were the glittery purple of Sparkles, Cuz! The man she called on was dressed in all black. He had silky silver shoulder-length hair that hung in his eyes. His chubby arm was draped around another mom when Priscilla called to him. He made a gesture of marital resignation and wobbled over to us. His nametag stated PHILIP.

"Honey, this is Sven Norberg," Priscilla said.

"Yes, I see," replied Philip. "Thanks for the smoke."

"This is *Kyle's* father."

"Oh," he said, looking at me as if I were a sudden obscenity in a children's book.

"We're Plea's parents," Priscilla said.

"Oh!" I cried, too avidly. I immediately reached for another smoke, offering them the pack again, which they refused with disgust, even though they'd both just finished smoking. "Plea is a lovely girl," I said.

"Yes." There seemed to be a threatening edge to Philip's words, though it was blunted under all the soft hair. "We think so. Your son doesn't seem to agree, however."

"Cut her off like that," Priscilla said. "Without even a word."

"She's been too upset to even go to school."

The words wrenched me. I had picked up the phone countless times and let my finger hover over the screen, but had been frozen mid-dial by the mental image of these very people (or their more aristocratic equivalents in my imagination).

"Kyle has been going through a weird phase," I said.

"Sounds more like a conversion to me," Priscilla said.

"No, I wouldn't go that far, wouldn't say 'conversion,' no."

"Not a very Christian way to act toward our daughter, in any case," Philip said, puffing up inside his turtleneck sweater.

"I agree," I said. "I completely agree. Of course we've been . . ."

"Right! Your wife," Philip said. The other parents had stopped chatting now, and there was an eerie silence in the now hot-boxed burnt orange, aqua, and charcoal bathroom. "What did they say happened to her, honey? They were saying she was kidnapped for a while."

"Or maybe even murdered," said Priscilla. "I'm pretty sure the word 'murder' came up."

"I am really *drunk*," one of the mothers said.

"Of course there are other possibilities," Philip said with an airy toss of his silver hair. "More obvious possibilities, closer to home."

"I'm late for class," I said through gritted teeth, snuffed my cigarette underfoot, and lunged for my escape. On my way out I couldn't resist a parting shot: "Hope you enjoyed the swingers' conference!" I said.

"We prefer the term *polyamorous*—" Philip's words broke on the tiles.

If I hurried, I could still make it to Art. Along the way I saw a couple of parents making out against a locker and a guy on the floor who was giggling wildly and looked like he had peed in his pants. A scornful custodian in a blue District 99 work shirt observed the scene, scribbling in a pocket notepad. When I asked him what he thought of this parent-teacher conference night, he said he was writing an epic satirical poem about it. Then he dipped his mop in a trough of suds and more or less shook it in my face.

14

O N THANKSGIVING MORNING, I SHAVED MY BEARD. IT HAD been a while. I hadn't yet smoked my first cigarette of the day and was exulting in the temporary delusion of health this gave me. By the time I went to work with the electric razor, I already regretted what I had done. My face is one of those faces that alarms when unsheathed. All the boyish insecurity of my features, the rodent-like need and juvenile worry, becomes instantly legible. There are certain faces that should be hidden by beards, and mine is one of them, I thought. Large clumps of hair wafted in the sink like tumbleweeds and lined the porcelain in wispy script. Examining myself in the mirror—pointy little Nordic chin, clear cheeks and bare jowls, Adam's apple— remorse overwhelmed me. I quickly fashioned a substitute beard out of shaving cream and hurried for my cigarettes.

There was a stiff dress shirt on a hanger and just mildly wrinkled pants by the bed. A hard, diagnostic sun shone through the window. Kyle was calling from downstairs. I avoided the full-length mirror, where Molly had so often mooned—I'd actually been *annoyed* at her for those momentary disappearances. My son waited on the landing, cradling a basket of crescent rolls and a bottle of wine. When he saw me, he chuckled, mouthing "Dad" as he pulled at his clean chin. I touched my face and came away with a handful of foam from my ghost beard. I brushed it off, and when we stepped outside, the cold wind stung my bare cheeks.

We were going to the Lillys' for Thanksgiving dinner. There, I said it: the Lillys. That deceptively gentle name is still a knot of pain to me. To my son, then, it was a song, a one-word weapon. "The *Lillys* invited me to Thanksgiving," Kyle said. "Pastor Lilly invited you too." It was as if a silent, powerful machine had kicked into motion behind my back, starting with the flier in our mailbox. We arrived at their home, somewhere in a surreal enclave of identical houses on a sculpted hillside; there were no trees. We drove from Sherwood Court to Sherwood Trail to Sherwood Street to Sherwood Lane. The gray van was parked in the driveway. I was welcomed in by a prim blonde named Cordelia, who handed me a business card with the name of their youth ministry and two black, eerily disembodied hands printed on it. As I made my doomed efforts to insert myself into my son's new life in the weeks to come, it was as if these two hands were pushing me; I felt their dark pressure on my back.

To her credit, Cordelia Lilly did not ask me about my wife. She only asked how I was and I managed to tell her, after a breath, that I was okay. Molly had become an awkward pause, a missed beat in conversation.

I'd had too much coffee that morning, so I asked for the restroom. With an accommodating smile, which suggested that this was a slightly grotesque request on my part, Cordelia led me down the hall, past framed pictures of the Lillys, standing among impoverished children in far-flung locales. The Bob Lilly of the photographs was a bearish, bearded man, his face weirdly out of focus. He looked steady and solid against the austere backdrops of Mumbai slums and wintry Balkan squares. The bathroom had salmon-colored wallpaper and a wide assortment of wipes and salves. There was a high window through which, after climbing onto the toilet seat, I could see Bob Lilly cutting wood out in the yard. He wore a farmer's flannel and the familiar chauffeur's cap. His axe swings were nonchalant, neatly splitting the logs. Isolated out there, he looked like some solitary woodsman from a Brueghel, negligible in the vast expanse of snow. I tried to imagine the deep pleasure the work was giving him, the clean sting of the cold. I climbed down from the toilet. The Lillys' bathroom smelled of cloves. With a burst of needling pain, I peed. As my urine splashed the bowl, golden and polluted, the reports of Lilly's axe echoed through Sherwood Forest.

WE GATHERED AROUND a smorgasbord of steaming, multicolored foods. Kyle took my hand, and Cordelia's, and began to pray. No one had asked him to do it and the ease with which he invoked the fictional Father disturbed me. The bright abundance was making me dizzy, and given how long I'd been living on junk and fumes, I wondered if I would be able to hold it down.

Toward the end of his prayer, Kyle said, "I pray that my dad can see the truth, even if it is too big for him to see right now."

"Pretty eloquent," said Bob Lilly, sawdust still on his shirt sleeves. "You may have a preacher on your hands."

"He has gravitas," Cordelia added.

"It runs in the family," I muttered. Gravitas, like some genetic curse. I released Kyle's hand a moment late. Forcing a spoon of sweet potato into my mouth, I told myself that I was grateful for all that I hadn't yet lost.

AFTER DINNER, UNDER the guise of "getting a breath of fresh air," I went out to the yard for a smoke. I told Cordelia that after all, I was out here in the purer suburban elements and it would be a shame to waste them. She frowned. She was the kind of woman to whom it was difficult to lie, I thought, lighting up as soon as I was clear of the house's sightline. My steps made a series of craters in the snow. The smoke, combined with the shock of cold air in my lungs, was sublime.

"Got another one of those, bucko?"

I turned around, somehow expecting to see my father, though it was inconceivable that my father would ask for a cigarette. Lilly was loping through the snow, kicking up powder in his haste.

"Really?"

"Sure, of course. But no telling Cordelia, bucko. If she smells it, just say I was out here, talking to you amid your fumes."

"Okay." I handed him one. "I'd like to nip this 'bucko' thing in the bud, if possible."

"Ohh."

I lit his smoke for him, careful not to singe his enviable beard with the lighter.

"Neat kid you've got." Lilly smiled. "Very serious, intense kid. But neat."

We blew out two contrails of smoke that faded instantly. The new houses on the hill looked massive and vacant.

"It's been a tough year," I said. "He's very vulnerable right now."

"He's in great shape, compared to me at that age," Lilly said. "Fifteen years old, I ran away, moved to an abandoned grain mill downtown. I was dropping acid at least twice a week. Used to go out to the mall, right when it opened, wander around in that labyrinth all day, stoned out of my mind. The first time I found Jesus it was when I woke up in the mall Dumpster, where my friends had left me for dead."

"That was good timing," I said.

He didn't pick up the tone—or, generously, he chose to ignore it. "It was, bucko, it was. But I lost him again later. Anyway, what was I saying? I'm lucky to be around at all. And to have Cordelia, who puts up with a lot. A lot more than you know." He dropped his half-smoked cigarette and kicked some snow over it. "It's no picnic, what you've been going through. Don't hesitate to call on us if we can help in any way, bucko."

"It's kind of you. I'm really doing fine, though."

"Sure you are. Sure you are. Come over here, I want to show you something."

Lilly took long, decisive strides over the bare slope. The snow had melted there and the grass had the look of a dry wound. I trailed behind huffing, Kyle's prayer ringing in my ears. Lilly pointed past the edge of the development to the faint rainbow-like glow of the highway's neon lights. "It's kind of beautiful, don't you think?"

"In a way," I said.

"Every night, before I pray," Lilly said, "I look out at those lights. And it just reminds me of all the world's junk. The sheer junkiness of it. Our church is off that highway too, but you wouldn't know. All you see are the hotels and chicken wings and showgirls. I'm getting to the point in my life where I'm thinking about my legacy. I want to leave something tangible behind. And one night when I was looking out, I just saw it. Three crosses soaring over I-99, leading the way to our church. It just came to me in a kind of vision."

"This wasn't a drug-induced vision?"

"Very funny, bucko." Lilly pointed an inspired finger into the distance, where the highway snaked off and diminished. "They're going to be three hundred feet high. You'll be able to see them from downtown, and from way out in New Arcadia. It's been a ton of work raising the money, but we're almost there. It's going to be beautiful."

He walked up the hill and gazed out. Behind him, the shadows of the saplings fell like dark hands in the plush, white snow.

THE GROUNDBREAKING CEREMONY for the new crosses was held two weeks later. To my surprise, Kyle asked me to come, so I didn't need to invoke the weather to justify my continued supervision. Conditions were, in fact, bad. I-99 was a smear of neon lights, the snowbanks black from exhaust. Small quantities of gray slush splashed up through the rusted frame of Molly's car. The only radio station that wasn't playing Christmas music was playing an absurdly laid-back jazz trio, its mellow bleats and xylophone taps inadequate against the night. I reduced it to a murmur. We were like two conscripts on a submarine, I thought, sharing the same cramped vulnerable silence. I turned off at the exit to FIRST CHURCH OF THE DIVINE PURPOSE. The slick exit ramp was steeper than I expected, and for a few unnerving seconds the car's tires lost traction. I rode it out, and after recovering control wondered if Kyle had noticed my mishap. I decided to say nothing and glanced over at him. My son regarded me doubtfully.

Behind a line of cautious, blinking vehicles we rolled onto the premises that had captivated him. The parking lot was a well-lit void in the winter dark. We parked far away from the church itself, a massive concrete dome that had been designed by Bernhard's professional and sexual rival, von Hartsig. Upon its completion Bernhard had written: "I congratulate von Hartsig on his enormous mushroom." On the other side of the lot was a one-room brick chapel, which announced itself as the F.C.O.D.P.'s original house of worship. A group of dour figures had gathered on the steps, dressed in worn, faded gray suits and dresses, each of them cradling an open, empty suitcase. Their eyes were intransigent and steely as the sky.

"Who are those people?" I asked Kyle.

"The Dissenters," he replied. "They worship there, in the old church."

I did not understand the source of the disagreement, exactly. We walked past them, toward the carnival tent and the movie premiere lights. Young girls in peacoats handed us candles and hot cider in paper cups.

It was an ordeal to keep my candle lit. The flame was small and feeble. I had to reignite it twice with my cigarette lighter. The tent was not providing much shelter, trembling over celebrants who stamped their feet and blew into their hands. Across the tent, I saw Cordelia Lilly waving and smiling. She managed to look elegant in earmuffs somehow. I waved back, but she had already turned away. In response to the snub, I lit a cigarette with my candle. When I turned to Kyle to see if I could get some idea of when the ceremony would begin, he had drifted to another part of the crowd.

The mayor of Sherwood Forest came up to give a brief speech. Swaddled in a red coat, she grappled with the microphone and her glasses kept fogging up. She clearly did not want to be here any more than I did. She delivered a few minutes of tepid oratory, then raised a huge key to the city. When she said Lilly's name there was a roar. The applause was shocking from such a small crowd—everyone must have been screaming at the top of their lungs. Lilly accepted the giant key and shook the mayor's hand. He was wearing a leather jacket over a big wool sweater that looked hand-knit. His corduroy pants billowed around his trunk-like legs. The applause held on, growing and feeding on itself. Near the front, Kyle was pumping his fist in the air along with a group of kids in big down coats.

Lilly stepped up to the microphone and cleared his throat. With his hair slicked back and his beard trimmed, he looked like a sepia-toned pioneer. In the candlelight his figure was richly shadowed. Two fluted speakers projected his words from the edges of the stage. As I moved to avoid a direct hit of his voice, I checked to see if I was blocking anyone's view, and I saw behind me, far beyond the tent, in the outlying darkness, the small group of Dissenters still standing on the steps of the old chapel with their open suitcases.

"Friends," Lilly said. "Tonight is the culmination of a long struggle. That struggle began one hundred and fifty years ago,

when my great-great grandfather, Georg Lula, ended his pil-
grimage in Trude." He paused and raised his right arm, extending the fingers of his hand; the shadow appeared as an engorged
black spider on the ceiling of the tent. "He and the others
stopped here because they saw a hand in the sky. They recognized the image at once, of course. In the medieval period it was
called the Powerful Hand. The fingers stood for each of the
apostles, and the thumb was our Savior. They understood the
message, although this was also a simple sign. The same sign a
policeman makes when directing traffic at an intersection. They
saw this hand on the same hill where we stand now, at the edge
of the city. The cloud blew apart but they stayed on.

"Now my great-great-grandfather, he believed, and I believe
as well, that the Second Coming is imminent. That is what we
have always believed and we long for this joyful event. The question
has been, how do we prepare ourselves for this transformation?
Do we make inroads into the city around us, adopting others
into our cause, or do we focus solely on the purification of our
own hearts?"

His voice swelled, and wherever I moved I could not avoid
its direct beam. The voice entered my body through every ori-
fice and infiltrated my corrupt veins and channels. In the back
of the tent I thought I saw Plea cowering, her hands cupping a
candle, her vast sunken eyes holding a glimmer of orange light,
but when she turned her head, she was a stranger. Lilly's next words
were directed to the Dissenters, pale and ghastly as ancestors,
on the chapel steps beyond the tent.

"Certainly we have been mocked. From the very begin-
ning, the Trudians did not understand us. The city that God
chose for us. They wrote us off, turned us into wild-eyed fanatics

in newspaper cartoons. And now the city itself has fallen on hard times. It is exposed to poverty, crime, decay, every form of depravity. The old, good people have fled and the new, bad people have arrived. So the story goes. Some of us have even welcomed these developments, as if our church might shine more brightly as the city around us becomes a dire morass, doomed beyond all measure."

There were distant cheers from the church steps. Suitcases raised high.

"But wait, my friends." He raised his hand again, the spider crawled on the ceiling. "Wait. I do not think we can applaud this turn of events. Because out there in the decaying city are lost human spirits, growing more lost with each passing day, as they walk down one street, turn a corner, and see only rows of lightless crumbling buildings that look terribly familiar, as if they will never change."

His eyes flickered over me and yes, my candle had gone out again. It was a windy night and the candles had clearly come from the bargain bin. For a moment I wondered if Lilly's pages had blown off the podium, because he seemed to have lost his place, or maybe it was just a long oratorical pause; but no, he'd paused to collect himself. When he addressed the crowd again there were tears glimmering in his beard.

"You see I can't just write those spirits off like debts on a ledger," he said, "because I was one of them. As lost as any of them. Ask Cordelia what today is. Why we chose this day for such a momentous event. She will tell you that it's our son's birthday." He lowered his head and candles were raised around the tent. "He would have been nine years old today, if I had been a better father, if I had not been as profoundly lost as I was.

There were no crosses by the highway leading to the church back then. But if there had been, if there had been crosses over the road in those days of pure blackness, I would have thanked God for giving me a sign so clear. Almost as clear as a hand across the sky."

Throughout the speech, the Sherwood Forest mayor had been gripping a large spade with apprehension. Now, amid wild applause, she forced the spade into the frozen ground. She turned over a small mound of dirt and handed the spade to Lilly. My son was right up front now, beaming, close to the laborers. With his thick arms Lilly had considerably more success than the mayor had. He pushed the spade down with his boot and turned out a substantial clump of earth with roots dangling from it. There were cheers and photo flashes. The mayor, eager to get home, quickly assembled a weary smile, but a disconsolate tremor lingered in Lilly's mouth as he considered the little grave he had dug.

AFTERWARD THE CROWD drifted toward the bright shoveled square of the parking lot, which was lined with illuminated lunch bags. The concrete dome of the F.C.O.D.P. loomed in the background, its imposing form indifferent to the flimsy trees Sunday scholars had planted in the acreage around it. The lot was full of teenagers in heavy coats, caps, and mittens. They unpacked bags and boxes from car trunks and sat them down on the icy asphalt. Some parents stood between two parked minivans, cooking brats on a miniature grill. The *Trude at Ten* news van was on the scene. Somewhere in the crowd I caught a glimpse of the girl who looked like Plea, wearing an army jacket and a stocking cap. Her cheeks were flushed bright red. When I ventured a tentative smile in her direction, she did not return it but her eyes lingered on me.

The teenagers, by candlelight, looked muffled and anonymous in their winter clothes, like miners darkened with dust and soot. The news cameraman seemed to recognize this and made a slow circuit around the parking lot filming them. After unloading his trunk, Lilly joined a group of burly fire-builders. I went for hot cider, grabbing a second for Kyle. The stack of logs grew to a tower. Guys in soft sweatshirts kept stuffing logs and firestarters in.

"So what exactly is going on here?" I asked Kyle, handing him the warm cup.

"Ever heard of a bonfire of the vanities, Dad?" he asked.

He'd brought two full paper grocery bags. I did not especially want to know what was in them. Kyle watched the progress of the firewood tower with intent, gleaming eyes. The tower grew so tall that one of the men had to climb on the back of a pickup cab to add the final logs.

Lilly nodded to the men, admiring the tower. He stepped to the center of the crowd. His sweater rippled in the cold wind. A cheer rose up from the crowd. One of Lilly's men struck a match and handed it to him. Lilly let it burn for a moment, holding it up to his face. A private smile formed on his lips, in the small circle of light from the match, the most visible point in the crepuscular parking lot.

Lilly solemnly cupped the match's small flame in his hand, turned to the tower of logs, and wicked some newspaper. The other men followed suit. Sparks flew up, a fiery counterpoint to the directionless snowflakes that fell. The fire took hold and for

a few moments all of us, even the newscaster, stood mesmerized
watching it. Then a young girl ran up to the fire with a teddy
bear and an armful of dolls. She threw them in, as the crowd
shrieked and whooped, and the cameraman filmed it all for *Trude
at Ten*. The taut plastic limbs of the dolls melted to syrup over
the logs. Someone threw in their record collection. Someone
else tossed in a pile of dirty magazines. The girl I'd mistaken for
Plea approached the fire with a white dress. In the light of the
flames she was clearly too thin, otherworldly-looking, nothing
like the girl I'd taken her for. The dress could have been for her
wedding, but she was too young. It was sternly stitched and heir-
loom-like in its simplicity. The girl took a last fond glance at it
before tossing it into the air—it lay, seemingly inflammable, on
the pyre for a moment, as if she had laid it out on a bed. Then
the lace collar curled inward, and the whole dress dissolved in
the fire, lingering as an ashen shadow for a moment before it
emerged as gray powder in the air. A blond kid in a reverse baseball cap, who I would not have taken as a reader at all, threw on
a shelf's worth of thick paperbacks. A model train set went in, a
sheaf of glossy posters. A fizzling television knocked over a couple of logs, destabilizing the whole rank bonfire, which was now
disgorging ten different kinds of smoke. Kyle was hanging back.
He had gathered it, all of the sheet music Molly had bought for
him, from the shopping bags. The programs from his recitals,
the pictures of him at the piano, the certificates awarding him
second or third place in local competitions. Now I knew why
he'd brought me here. I wanted more than anything to try to
stop him. He was destroying something that was not finished,
that had not ended. But my body didn't move. He ran to the fire
and flung Beethoven, Brahms, and Schubert—the scores flailed

weakly over the fire for a moment like lame birds, before their papery wings caught fire, and they fell into the combustion of dolls, records, and porn magazines. When Kyle turned around, backlit by the fire, his face was bright and flushed, and he looked directly my way, his face screwed up in a triumphant, bitter smile. I contemplated the bag at my feet. I pulled out the recital programs, the notes in Molly's hand, the certificates and photographs. I felt like I was defacing the paintings in my favorite museum. Kyle nodded to me, gestured toward the fire. Everything moved very slowly, the flames included. I gathered the tainted relics. I took two steps toward the fire, pushed the papers from my chest, and let them scatter, inhaling the smoke of my life.

15

RUDE MISSED ITS LIBRARIES. THEY HAD SERVED A NUMBER of crucial civic functions that became apparent only in their absence. First of all, libraries had sheltered large numbers of stray individuals who, with nowhere else to go, now invaded office building lobbies, banks, food courts, and other quasi-public spaces. Idle and bearded men, disconnected from the library's webbed computers, turned their attentions to the office workers of downtown with unwelcome results. Some of the individuals were ill in the head. It turned out—and how could the mayor have foreseen this?—that certain deep psychological needs were being filled by the library. Disorders and manias were being held at bay. Say you were a severe obsessive- compulsive with no income: could anything be as satisfying as placing hundreds of requests for library materials, followed by a visit to a branch to pick up some of these items, inquire about the library's failure to supply others, and to challenge the inevitable fines and delinquencies on your library card, while at the same time placing further requests and so on ad infinitum? Could anything else so beautifully create the illusion of control? Such a person, left unmoored, had no choice but to begin patronizing other governmental agencies, such as City Records, Social Security, the License Bureau, and the Parks Board. Employees of these agencies began to chafe at the sheer amount of bizarre attention they were receiving. It was not only the fringe element that suffered. Young children no longer had a place to let loose. The elderly, deprived of their romance novels and audiobook mysteries, succumbed to ennui. And of course there were the librarians themselves. They were suspected of vandalism at the former Coty Branch Library, which had been converted into a luxury loft for a former Fuller aide. Who else would have had the motivation to spray-paint EX LIBRIS in bright red across the front windows? The core group at Central, nicknamed the Trude Thirteen by their many admirers, had proven intransigent and resourceful. They had become local heroes. They were entertaining the public, and no one but the mayor wanted to see them defeated.

Fuller looked defensive and aggrieved at his televised press conference. Dressed down in a polo shirt and gray blazer, he gripped both hands on the podium before him, as if to gain a firmer purchase on his office. While admitting that the library shutdown had been botched, he defended it in principle, arguing that the library was a "soft and socialist institution" and that it had no role in the more muscular Trude he was building. He cited increased investment, the renovation of distressed properties in the downtown area, low unemployment rates, and the imminent arrival of two lucrative conferences in the city, the National Numismatist's Convention and the Semi-Automatic Gun Show. When he opened the floor to questions, however, the press did not take the bait, nor did they respond to his attempts to steer the conversation toward more promising subjects, instead peppering him with wry inquiries into the library situation. Had the mayor had an unpleasant experience at the library as a child? (No, he preferred bookstores. He believed authors should be compensated for their work.) Did his policy have anything to do with the recently revealed delinquency on his library card—$12.50 in overdue fines and a romance novel returned in waterlogged condition? ("It was that way when I got it," the mayor barked.) Was he purposely trying to withhold information from the public? ("Information is a dubious commodity," he replied cryptically.) Wasn't it cruel to cut the gas at the Central Library, especially given the run of subzero temperatures expected in Trude next week? ("The Trude Thirteen are terrorists," he responded, to widespread laughter, "and must be dealt with as such.") Did he plan to persist to the end? (In a headline-making quote, Fuller said, "This will not last much longer. I have them in a half nelson.") A wary aide tapped Fuller's shoulder and whispered into his ear. The mayor stepped back from the podium with a look of great relief. "Thanks for your interest, gentlemen," he said, apparently oblivious to the fact that there were at least a dozen women in the room.

One of the oft-remarked ironies of the library situation was that this building, once the sine qua non of accessibility, was now one of the most exclusive places in Trude. The Trude Thirteen were obviously still receiving supplies through the leaks in the police blockade, but this traffic was covert and dusky. By day the windows were shaded and the staircase taped off, the two gilded owls asleep below. This sequestered quality of the library had been troubling me lately. The Central Library had closed its doors only days after Molly's disappearance, after all, and now that there were signs she was alive—the missing nightgown, Breeze's acrostic, the Oracle's dream—I pictured her sometimes, in my weaker moments, huddled among yellowing tomes in the vast, subterranean stacks.

THAT BOOK OF Molly's, the one she had been reading during our last night together, turned up in the last place I would have looked for it. Already late for work, I was in the midst of a frantic hunt for my keys when I found the missing book wedged beneath the seat cushion of my very own armchair. Hard to believe that I had been sitting on this important artifact all these months, but the merits of the old armchair had betrayed me in this case. The ancient cushion was so well-molded, so firm yet accommodating, that I'd never suspected a foreign object might be sunk deep in its embrace. The book was covered with dust and crumbs, and a couple of dimes were stuck to the jacket. It was unmistakably the book my wife had been reading the night before she disappeared; I remembered its slim shape, its black-and-white cover depicting a hippieish woman with long dreadlocks contemplating a female statue that strongly resembled her. The title, which I had not noticed before, was *Medusa Is Looking Pretty Today*, a collection of short stories. I had to catch my breath when I read the name of the author, because she was someone we knew—or more accurately, someone Molly knew. Cassandra Clark had been the librarian at Trude U when we were undergraduates, and at the time I met Molly there were rumors going around that the two of them were involved. As Molly explained it later, there had been a misunderstanding. The photo inside the dust jacket showed a distinguished black woman with buzz-cut hair, the large hoop earrings of the era, and a knowing, pretty smile.

What did she understand that I did not? And was this some kind of message Molly had left me, this reminder of the time before we met, before we had any connection to one another? The book seemed to open onto a void The only answer that *Medusa* had for me was scrawled on the title page: *Molly, see p. 134.* That was it—no signature, no endearment. When I checked the table of contents, the page number 134 was listed next to a story called "The Defect."

I located my keys at last, sped to the strip mall, heard the obligatory rebuke from Boggs, and settled in behind the front desk to read. Two clients, two sprained knees and a broken nose between them, watched me from the lobby chairs. They could never experience the very precise pain Cassandra Clark's sentences were causing me, the tanned paper and fogged print. The reception desk was partially shielded from the lobby by a row of fresh lilies, delivered weekly by a man in a purple visor. This floral border insulated me from Boggs's clientele. Their moans of discomfort reached me sweetly scented. I was not a big fan of those weirdly funereal flowers, but Boggs kept a standing order. The strong floral perfume filled my nostrils as I read, so much so that I unjustly imported a countertop bouquet to the provincial library where Cassandra Clark's story was set. The protagonist of "The Defect" was a nameless librarian who embodied almost every conceivable cliché of the profession. She wore cardboardy tweed suits even in summer, glowered at children through thick glasses, and amused herself by reorganizing the card catalog (the story was set in the 1950s). The only pleasure for this otherwise despotic soul was to converse with a certain young redheaded housewife who visited the library every Wednesday afternoon to browse romance novels. The young housewife (with her equally familiar 1950s wardrobe of sundresses and cheerful cardigans) was married to a businessman in the small provincial town. The husband was not particularly relevant to the tale at hand and was depicted in a few broad strokes. The housewife seemed cheerful on her library visits, and often stayed to chat. For the librarian, these conversations were the only balm in a life of unvarying, tweedy sadness. She took the new romance novels home with her to read the night before she would suggest them to the housewife, and as she perused them, stretching her aging and untouched body out in the tub, the librarian liked to think that the two of them were communing illicitly via the shared books, which provided a secret fulfillment the vague husband could not. Then one week, accidentally or half-accidentally, the librarian left a grocery list of her own inside one of the novels she checked out to the housewife. As the housewife left the small provincial library in a flurry of 1950s pink linen, the librarian made the horrifying, then increasingly galvanizing realization. The librarian spent several sleepless nights imagining the housewife reading that ascetic list: bread, milk, chicken thighs, grapes, spinach, oatmeal. For the first time, the librarian had left a trace of herself within the shared fantasy of the romance novels. When the housewife returned the next week and made small talk as usual, the librarian concluded that the housewife approved of her accidental intrusion into the romance novel's forbidden world. Each week now, the librarian would make some small alteration or addition to the books. Contradicting every premise she had learned in library school, her whole body thrilled with violation. The librarian might change the name of a character from "John" to "Joan" with a black pen and a bottle of Wite-Out. She added lines of dialogue to the ends of chapters, revised kisses, edited embraces. The housewife continued to visit the library, but she began to regard the librarian with wariness. She no longer discussed weather or trivial events in the provincial town, and she began to take out other kinds of books, presidential biographies for example, accepting the romances only at the librarian's absolute insistence. The librarian had transgressed too far, and she could not turn back. In a frenzy, she tore a whole chapter from the last romance novel she would ever hand to the housewife, adding her own typed chapter in its place. She put her own feelings for the housewife into the mouth of a brooding Scottish highlander named Fergus. She pasted the chapter in with book glue and left it on the counter to dry. The librarian waited behind the flowerless desk on the appointed day, the book shaking in her grip. The lovely housewife faltered but accepted it. The next week was torture for the librarian—she hardly slept, and her work at the library fell off. She made errors, misshelved books, forgot the names of authors, and generally could think of nothing but the lovely young redheaded housewife who had so unjustly married the boring businessman. When the housewife returned at last, the librarian almost fainted. Her body felt like it was being pierced by a thousand pins. The housewife's face was flushed almost to the hue of her hair. She slammed the book down on the counter. "This book is defective," the housewife simply said, turned, and left the library for the last time. The librarian sat looking at the book for a few minutes. She did not open it to see if the chapter she had rewritten was still inside. The word *defective* rang through her head as she vacated her desk and walked out through the back door. The librarian crossed a parking lot full of "fat beached cars" to throw the book out in the Dumpster; as she did so she looked down the street at the small and now desolate town, which we were seeing along with her for the first time, its diminishing vistas, its white houses "shrinking into the distance." I was disappointed at first with this ending, then realized that this sensation had been brilliantly engineered by Cassandra Clark, who wanted me to wonder whether the "defect" was in the librarian, the book she gave to the housewife, the provincial town where the story was set, or in the story itself that I was reading.

THE CENTRAL LIBRARY was definitely not open for business. Even in downtown's nighttime lull, however, there was a lingering aura of grandeur to it. The imposing windows were obscured by hundreds of posters promoting banned books. Behind the front gate, a pair of librarians in ski masks were on patrol, their shotguns resting by their sides, staffing a de facto outdoor reference desk that no one was brave enough to approach. The police also maintained their presence, if somewhat diminished. Half a block down from the entrance, a squad car idled with its lights on, throwing a monotonous magic lantern show against the library's granite walls. McCready and the Oracle leaned on the hood of their cruiser. They were now wearing dark blue polos, dark jackets, and khakis. It looked like their own shadows had been promoted above them. The Oracle had been chipping ice off the windshield but the scraper lay just beyond the reach of his hand. He was still wearing his racer shades.

"What brings you here, Norberg?" McCready called. "Want to check out a book? Too bad."

"Actually I was hoping to see a librarian," I said.

"That would be strictly against regulations," McCready observed neutrally. He raised a wadded and frozen handkerchief to his runny nose. "Which one do you want to see? Not that it matters."

"Cassandra Clark."

"Wow," McCready said. "Straight to the top for Norberg."

"There would be extensive frisking involved with that," the Oracle leered.

"You're not still looking for your wife, by any chance?" asked McCready.

I nodded curtly, annoyed.

"There are certain limits on what we should be interested in," the Oracle said. He dropped his ice scraper on the hood of the car. "These past few months may not have been my finest hours in law enforcement."

"No kidding," McCready muttered.

"But I would advise you," the Oracle continued, "to abandon this. And I say that in a friendly way, not in a veiled-threat sort of way. I would call this case cold. An endeavor of futility and embarrassment. Look what has happened to Detective McCready and myself. If we had never been involved with your wife's so-called case, we would never have been forced to employ the unorthodox methods that angered our superiors. We would not have been tabbed for the bête noire of all assignments, library security."

"Two words," McCready explained. "Internal audit." He scowled. "This is gas station coffee, Norberg."

It took me a few moments to get it. "How much?"

"I'm thinking whatever's in your pockets," McCready said. "And that's just for the request. No refunds if she doesn't want to see you."

$27.66 got me to the service door. As I waited in the snow, McCready called out: "See if you can get us something to read! And something with some action."

"Maybe even a corpse," the Oracle added.

AFTER A FEW minutes the door opened and a thin man in a red ski mask pulled me into the library. He pushed a handgun into my back, frisked me with masseur's fingers, and affixed my blindfold. The air was stale. The blindfold reeked of the last inductee's sweat. He pushed me through corridors, gently nudging me with his gun muzzle. He led me up a flight of stairs and restored my sight. I looked to him, the former reference assistant or circulation clerk, for some acknowledgment of the intimacies we'd just shared. The red ski mask covered everything except two coldly intelligent eyes, refracted through bifocals.

I found myself in the main foyer in front of the request counter. Central's collection had long ago outgrown its facilities, and the vast majority of its material was held in subterranean stacks. Patrons left their requests at the long oak counter, then sat to wait like travelers at a bus station while the slips were conveyed to the pages below via pneumatic tubing. Here I was at midnight in a room that couldn't have been much warmer than fifty degrees thanks to our mayor, yet in many ways things were just as they had been—the humming elementary school clock, the high ecclesiastical windows, the clerk at the counter looking

overeducated. Bulked up by at least three sweaters, she was reading *Opera as Drama* by flashlight.

"You're Molly's husband," she said matter-of-factly. She
paused before saying: "You were a fortunate man."

"Yes," I said. "The past tense is key there."

"Extremely lucky," she repeated. "I hope you realized it."

She climbed the stairs, the taps of her flats echoing
through the cavernous corridors. I slumped back against one
of the wooden pew-like benches, suddenly tired. I clutched
Cassandra Clark's book to my chest as if to warm it. Half an
hour or more passed—the shadows shifting against the arch-
ways, the moonlight glazing the ceiling's chiseled paeans to
knowledge and culture. I could not have felt more medieval,
more in the dark. The high beams of a freight truck outside
streaked across the mosaic image of a scholar: he peered down
at my shivering body through his monocle. The vast rooms
with their rows of gray reference books had the dark immensity
of graveyards.

At last the librarian returned, her circle of flashlight preceding her across the marble floor. She brought the masked sentry who went through the motions, with less gentleness this
time. He pushed me up a stairway and down a long hall. A door
creaked open and I landed in a surprisingly comfortable chair.

The sentry then retreated to his post. That left only
Cassandra Clark and I, by firelight, in matching high-backed
chairs. She'd held up well: her graying bangs and horn-rims
framed the same dusky face that I remembered from the college circ desk. Cassandra cracked the knuckles of hands that
had passed me weathered editions of Keats and Byron twenty
years ago, for the Dead Ends of the Romantic Poets seminar.

The wrinkles around her eyes must have been recent. She somehow looked dignified in leg warmers and blue rabbit slippers.

"You must be disappointed in my outfit," she said. "Molly told me you're a fan of librarian movies. Have you seen *Indecent Reference?*"

"Um—" So she had known about the drawer, after all.

"I was actually a consultant on that . . . film," Cassandra said. "The director, fellow by the name of Van Voyage, felt that a scrupulous realism would enhance the . . . effect." She looked for confirmation, crossing her thin bundled legs.

"Realism is important in these matters," I murmured.

"I provided some uncredited script doctoring for the notorious overdue fines scene," she said. "Ah well. A sad man really, Mr. Voyage. High hopes for himself."

The room had a darkened elegance—I could only just make out the brass lamps, the portraits of Trudian patriarchs in heavy frames. The patriarchs' memoirs had been pulled from the shelves and lay stacked on the mantle. Cassandra took one down, did a cursory flip-through, and tossed it on the fire, the ribbon bookmark going up in a brief tail of flame.

"You hate to do it," Cassandra said. "However unnecessary a book may be, it's a harsh form of withdrawal."

"The mayor must be laughing somewhere."

"I hope so," she said. "I hope it is amusing *someone*."

We sat quietly for a long moment. Tall, complicated shadows swirled from the flames in the grate. Finally I told her, in a mock-casual tone, as if I were just some library patron chatting her up, about my reading of "The Defect" earlier in the day and the fact that Molly had been reading it the night before she disappeared. Either from hearing me mention her work or Molly's name, Cassandra contracted.

"I don't think I could reread that story," Cassandra said at last. "I mean it was so amateur, so transparent, so . . ."

"Autobiographical?" I asked.

She sighed. "Look, Sven, what happened between your wife and me happened twenty years ago. It meant very little to her and very much to me. Or maybe I should say for her it ended, for me it went on."

"I thought the story held up pretty well," I said. "I guess Molly did too. Have you seen her recently by any chance?"

The librarian nodded and removed her glasses, which had fogged from her proximity to the fire. "She called a month before . . . in April. It was April Fool's Day, in fact. I thought she was kidding. I met her a couple of times for lunch, but it was only in the capacity of an old friend giving advice."

"Perhaps you advised her to hide out here with you?"

Cassandra shook her head, still wiping her glasses.

"Or to abandon her family without a word?"

"Of course not," Cassandra said, in a conclusive tone that would have subdued the patrons. Then, more softly, she continued: "There was a time when I despised you, Sven. That was only because I kept asking myself how she could ever have chosen you. I must have been an idiot. The answer was simple: you were a man, she thought she could change you. You were an interesting problem case, this shy withdrawn paranoiac nobody understood. 'I'm his only human connection,' she told me once."

She must have caught my skeptical look in the darkness. "The idea that librarians are more knowledgeable than ordinary people—well, that's just a myth, I'm afraid," she said.

147

"What about Martin Breeze's column?"

There was a dense silence. "I saw it," she said at last. "Our government documents guy is a puzzle freak."

"And what do you make of it?"

Cassandra swept her glasses through the air. "I took it to mean that she is alive," she offered cautiously. She closed her eyes, lay back against the chair. "To be honest I was reluctant to meet Molly when she called," she said. When Cassandra spoke again it was half to herself. "I'd worked so hard to erase her. What else could I have done? I censored her, banned her from my mind. I had made her disappear already, years before she physically . . . Do you see? I am a strong-willed person and I like to believe I have some control over what comes in and out of my life, but making Molly disappear was probably the hardest thing I ever did. When she called me last spring it was like, what? You're doing *what* to me, barging into my life again? But then I saw how unhappy she was."

I swallowed. "Did she say anything about . . ."

"She sounded *restless* to me," Cassandra said. "There were people who wanted her out of the opera, as I'm sure you know. But there was also this, I don't know, a kind of existential restlessness if that makes any sense. She kept saying she didn't want to die here. But we all feel like that sometimes, right? Who wants to consider dying in Trude? Nobody. That doesn't mean she could just leave you and Kyle."

"Exactly," I said, the word coming out in a cloud of breath. "Those are my thoughts exactly. That would be impossible."

"Then again, I was never an especially good judge of her character." The fire was out. Cassandra lit a candle and pulled a wool afghan over her shoulders.

Our breaths mingled, exhalations from two mouths that had kissed Molly's.

"Sorry it's gotten so cold," Cassandra said.

I told her it was all right, explaining about my January birthday, the frigid childhood ski outings my father had taken me on, my low body temperature. I told her how Molly used to call me Iceberg.

"She used to call me Four-Eyes," the head librarian replied wistfully, restoring her horn-rims to their perch and blinking behind the icy lenses.

16

THE RINGSTRASSE STILL MADE QUITE AN IMPRESSION AS YOU approached on I-99, the whitewashed spirals of concrete looming under the night sky. Bernhard had envisioned it as the locus of a second city, a new downtown for an ideal Trude to replace the declining original. He wanted the mall to look Greek, noting wryly that the Oracle at Delphi was once surrounded by junk dealers and souvenir sellers. The exterior of the mall was blinding in its early years. It gave off an almost holy radiance. Later in the seventies, it became a haven for drug abusers and its white walls were gradually covered with slogans, oblique verse, taunts, vows, band names, tags, secret codes. Mall security began letting the graffiti slide, and the densely scripted exterior wall became another of the mall's attractions, even opening itself to prayers in time. The orchestral pavilion was abandoned, the hanging gardens converted to parking.

"My buildings," Bernhard wrote in his *Memoirs*, "are like rebellious children who have grown up to disappoint and betray me."

I had lost my sense of agency during the past months. I no longer "made plans," it seemed, but instead found myself conscripted into events. This could be the only explanation of why I found myself in Lilly's van, en route to a benefit show given by the young bard Sebastian, staged at the mall's labyrinthine heart. The Christian rocker had been closing in on me, starting as unpleasant murmurings in Kyle's room, then appearing shirtless on his wall, and now blaring from Lilly's excellent stereo. The concert was a coup for the cross project and for Lilly, who was friends with Sebastian's agent back in his preterite pot smoking days. Rolling into the Ariadne lot, Lilly reminisced about defiling the mall's concrete exterior, the acrid blast of fresh spray paint.

As we walked in the west entrance, I had to admit that Bernhard's detractors had a point. It wasn't very successful as a mall. The vast echoing chambers, the blank concrete, exposed the ultimate hollowness of the retail urge. This was especially the case in the mall's outer rings, where the large department stores were housed. One tiled path might lead you directly to a perfume counter, while another curved around to a copper statue of Hermes presiding over a dried-up fountain full of rusty pennies. We tried to stay on course, but the inner rings of the mall were closed off for the show. As we approached the cordon, the crowd thickened with sullen loiterers, parents with raised fingers trying to strike a deal, weirdly overage and overweight male lurkers. "Three tickets, please, please, *please*," a group of scantily clad twelve-year-olds shouted in our direction, their voices hormonally coiled. We handed our tickets to a mall cop and were frisked by a security guard in an unflattering yellow T-shirt. As I watched Bob Lilly move through the crowd of his making, slapping palms, clapping shoulders and backs, whispering into

upturned ears, I realized I had underestimated the man upon
first meeting him. Lilly crept up on you. Everything the guy said
sounded a note sharp to me, but there was no question he was
an operator, out there fighting for souls, using whatever tools
the culture had to offer him. Lilly was decked out for the concert
in a gray hoodie, a frayed jean jacket, and a pair of vintage
bell-bottom cords. As Lilly worked the crowd I wondered why
someone so high up the F.C.O.D.P. totem would make so much
fuss over Kyle. There was no purely practical reason for it, but
you couldn't doubt, watching the two of them together, that they
had a personal bond. A stranger looking on would have taken
Lilly for the father, and me for the interloper. The crowd was
making me dizzy, like it always did, as we walked toward the
mall's center. This couldn't have been the kind of cultural event
Bernhard envisioned.

THE STORES BECAME more eccentric as you went in. There was
a shop that sold soap shaped like celebrity torsos, a mapmaker
peddling joke globes and plots of cities that didn't exist, one that
sold defective merchandise, and another that offered only mod-
els or reproductions of other commodities. Many owners stood
outside their stalls pitching to the passing throngs of Sebastian
fans. We passed Perlmutter's, where I'd purchased the Bernhard
autobiography and most of Kyle's Christmas presents—some of
the old modernist and existentialist classics I'd stooped and
scowled over in high school. Perlmutter's offered them in used
scholarly editions. At Clara's desk was an angry bespectacled
man with a widow's peak. The bookstore had a dimming aura of
obsolescence.

The hedge labyrinth, usually tranquil relative to the rush of the mall, was crammed. People had lined up ten deep against the walls, packed so tightly together that I was sure that some fire code was being violated. Sebastian fans had filtered into the labyrinth itself, from which the view was not good, but boyfriends were hoisting girlfriends on their shoulders, and others were clambering onto the hedges, their hair wet from the mist that poured down in clouds every fifteen minutes. There were two levels of balcony on either side, but these areas had been long filled by Sebastian fans who'd been waiting for hours. He could easily have filled a stadium, but had insisted on playing this space, which he hoped would enhance his "mythos." Or so I had read in a *Trumpet* column by Martin Breeze, whose distinctive battered brown leather jacket I recognized from far away.

Breeze looked nervous, his longish lock of gray hair combed to the side. His paunchy body was easy to pick out amid the svelte teens. He wore thick-framed bifocals that gave his eyes an aquatic look. Breeze hitched up his leather sleeve and checked his watch. He was a man out of place, always, wanting to get back to his computer, where he could transmute his displacement into scathing verbs. I wove through the young believers. Wielding their pocket electronica, they took pictures and conferred by phone. Breeze didn't recognize me right away, or maybe he was just shocked to meet me on the scene.

"Norberg." He looked me over wearily. "You chaperoning tonight?"

"In a way."

"I wish this little divo would get it over with," Breeze said. He eyed me again. "I saw you on the news the other day. Some sort of ceremonial book burning. I was pretty surprised to see you'd gone fundie, but it makes sense, considering what you've been through."

"Actually," I said, leaning close to Breeze's ear, "it was Kyle, my son, who was behind all that. I was . . ."

"Chaperoning."

"Yes."

"You haven't returned my calls," Breeze said.

"You called?"

He nodded. "You seemed to be getting into it," he said. "I mean the book burning, on the news. I sympathize. At some point it is just easier to accept someone else's metaphysics. It's too tiring to forge a personal theology. And if everyone did . . . well, imagine the chaos." He watched a couple of young girls jostle for position on a hedgerow. Breeze mused, "Is a personal theology even possible? Or does it amount to the same terminal paradox as a private language?"

I frowned. "You called?"

"Yes, you should check your messages." Breeze scanned the auditorium, as if he was about to mention something confidential. The crowd was about 75 percent teenage girls. "It was something Molly said during our interview. Something that got edited out."

At that moment I was blinded from behind by two small hands.

"Guess who."

Plea wrapped her arms around my neck and exhaled a mist of liquory breath that enveloped us. She wore Molly's Rotting Kisses T-shirt and the black sweatpants I'd lent her two months ago. The shirt had lost its shape, the sweatpants stretched to their limit by Plea's hips. The outfit was so unsettling that I lost my place in the conversation.

"I . . . perhaps we could talk later," Breeze stuttered.

"Introduce me to your friend, Norberg."

I did and the two shook hands. I felt certain that Breeze could read it all, the sex, the infatuation, the broken code in my being. His expression seemed quizzical and congratulatory all at once. "Plea is our local baker's apprentice," I told Breeze, feeling a slight buzz from this irrelevant detail, as if I'd just lifted some meaningless trinket from one of the department stores. Plea squeezed my hand out of Breeze's view. "Martin's the music critic for the *Trumpet*, an old friend," I added, lying again. As Plea pulled at my sleeve, Breeze handed me his business card. He wrote down a date and time under his name. "Come see me after the holiday," Breeze said, as Plea pulled me away from him. We flashed our wristbands to security and went out of the auditorium, through a door and down the hall. I followed her thoughtlessly. Her boot heels clacked and echoed off the walls. She was taking me toward the bathrooms, I realized. They weren't easy for just anyone to find. In fact, in all of Bernhard's buildings the bathrooms were tucked away as reluctant concessions to human weakness. The Traumhaus residents all had their own bathrooms but it had taken me months to discover the public restroom in the place, set off at the back like an outhouse. The Opera House hid theirs up by the second tier balcony, an architectural quirk not much appreciated by its elderly and hobbled patrons, and you can imagine the line during a Wagnerian intermission.

The women's lounge was halfway down the hall. Plea took me through the door, her grip almost painful now. The room was brightly lit: it featured pink furniture and a vanity lined with bare lightbulbs. The sink was stocked with various exfoliating soaps and small glass bottles of scent. This was not a kingdom I had ever been meant to enter. Molly had not appreciated it, that time I'd gone into her dressing room.

I didn't resist as she pushed me into the stall. Plea kissed and groped me and I responded in kind. I told her I'd missed her, and it was the truth. My wife's workout clothes rippled from her heaving body, giving my arousal an undercurrent of dread. It was only when she knelt on the tile and unzipped my pants that I felt the scene skipping out of control, like a strip of celluloid running off the reels. In the interests of completeness, I should say that it felt too fast. In fantasy these motions are languorous and relaxed, but Plea was handling me with a sort of brisk violence. It wasn't bringing pleasure. I felt like a boss. She was at work, going through a set of motions mechanically. Soon after this realization filtered through my body and everything went dry, I heard sounds from the stall next to us.

"It's okay," I said. "You can stop."

Her head fell on my thigh and rested there. She still held me in her right hand, while her left hand wrapped around my leg, and I stroked her hair. The Rotting Kisses T-shirt had torn at the shoulder, exposing a frayed and grandmotherly bra strap.

"I'm sorry," I said, lifting Plea into my arms.

Back in the labyrinth-auditorium, the crowd was growing impatient for the arrival of Sebastian and they clapped out a steady 4/4. I numbly read the message on the inside of the stall door: PLEASE DISPOSE OF SANITARY NAPKINS IN THE CORRECT RECEPTACLE (THEY STOP UP THE PLUMBING!). Beneath that someone else had scrawled, in the same accusatory capitals, THERE IS NO USE IN KILLING ONESELF; ONE ALWAYS DOES IT *TOO LATE*.

We were not alone in there. There was a woman in the neighboring stall crying. Someone had deceived her and left her flailing and unsure, perhaps. Or she was feeling old and flabby and formless. Who was to say? There were two rhythms, the rhythm of the claps and the sound of her sobs, and they were slightly staggered, or syncopated, as Molly would have put it. And I wished I had not thought of the word *syncopated* just then, because I was reminded of precisely how far I had drifted from the context in which that word had meaning. It was a floating signifier adrift in the perfumed air. There were scrapes, noises. The women were filing in now, forming a line. I heard their whispered complaints. I saw their white tapered ankles beneath the stall door. Someone, the sobber or us, would have to go on. I unlatched the door just as the auditorium broke into riotous applause.

17

THE PLASTIC TREE SLUMPED BY THE WINDOW, STRUNG WITH decrepit ornaments and a string of colored lights. Somehow I had pictured it looking different, before I'd found the supplies in the closet and dragged them out, before I'd stacked Kyle's parcels there, wrapped in old cartoon pages from the *Trumpet*. Christmas was a holiday that got harder to sustain as time went on; that was a lesson worth teaching. The boxes shrunk and ceased to glow and meant less when you opened them. Kyle dutifully uncovered the existentialist classics I'd purchased for him at Perlmutter's, books whose plain covers and yellowed pages drably proved their seriousness.

"Have you even read all these books, Dad?" Kyle said.

"Most of them," I said. "I read them a long time ago, when I was your age, and I've forgotten a lot, of course, but I learned—"

"Thanks." He flipped a few pages of Camus's *The Fall*, evidently unimpressed by the scabrous and richly ironic narration promised on the back cover.

Kyle turned a few hurried pages, looking for a signpost in the woods of print. Some dust might have come up in the process, but I believe he exaggerated his coughing fit.

I was missing, among other things, the smell of pine. Years ago, in times that now seemed impossibly remote, I would drive out to New Arcadia and buy a real tree from a plaid-shirted tough who would strap it to the roof of the car. Molly was bothered by the scattered pine needles, so we bought the artificial tree, which had itself become less pretty and functional with time, exactly as if it were real. There was something to be said for not pretending.

Kyle was at the window, making no attempt to conceal the fact that he was waiting on Lilly's van, counting the minutes until it arrived.

"Well, thanks, Dad," he said, without turning around. "I guess it's good to know your enemy."

"Your enemy?" I said. "Your *enemy*?"

He snorted. "I know you think life is pointless, but why do you want me to think it's pointless too? I didn't know it was something you tried to convert people to."

"That's not my position," I said. "I don't think that."

"Really?" He turned, and I could see a second mirrored Kyle in the window. The face gave me a watery sneer. "What is the point, then?" He paused. "As you see it."

"As I see it," I said. The words were not readily available. Kyle watched me triumphantly as I fumbled for my worldview. "As I see it, the point is to endure as much shit as you can without any illusions."

Kyle stood there for some time looking out to the cul-de-sac, still accompanied by his dim twin. He seemed to be considering various rebuttals. Finally he laughed, and said: "You know, Bob is so *totally right* about you." And, leaving this statement to hang, letting me steep in its cryptic air, Kyle went to the basement to collect his things. I wanted to ask him what he meant but as it turned out, I never got the chance.

BEFORE I KNEW it the sky's fade had begun, lowering the curtain on another brief and halfhearted midwinter day. You could feel buried in a building, especially your own house, I thought. I threw on my coat and walked outside, hoping that the cold would brace me. I set off with no destination in mind, hitching up my collar for extra anonymity as I walked the residential streets. The neighbors were crowded around tables, eating, singing. Some of their young were out, sledding down their sloped lawns or building snowmen and forts. (Bernhard had developed a late fascination with children's snowmen, thousands of which he photographed in his last years. Some claimed this showed a softening of his lifelong misanthropy, though it was just as likely that in these first crude architectural attempts, he sought to understand himself and his own compulsion to build.)

The snow was piled in big, soft banks on the curb, along the driveways. I walked down the icy sluice of the street. Last Christmas had not been so long ago. The three of us had driven to a Methodist church downtown, and Molly had sung "Once in Royal David's City." I had listened to her sing and I had listened to the Methodist minister's sermon, and afterward I'd shaken hands with my neighbors feeling something like real warmth and goodwill toward them. Molly and Kyle had been fighting about something, piano probably. Kyle had the expression Molly and I called "the POW look," but he had put on a decent-looking cardigan sweater and was enduring the proceedings. Kyle had not looked at all susceptible to the sermon, the minister's Christmas soft pitch, and when Molly sang from the balcony above and behind me, I did not even look back—that's how certain I was that it would all continue. Her voice, his reluctant presence.

The irregularly placed streetlights let their pools of yellow fall in the snow. I turned into a lane that was somewhat unfamiliar to me, the boughs of overhanging elms obscuring the sign. I took a left and started uphill, toward a clearing. I slipped a couple of times on my way up, skidding backward on the ice. The motion lights of three houses converged in a pale circle, though as far as I could tell there were no lights on inside the houses. They looked uninhabited, shrouded by trees. The cul-de-sac was oddly bright, one of those Midwestern blank spots aliens might choose for an abduction. The bright gravel circle seemed like a proscenium stage, where I was expected to climb and deliver an address I had not rehearsed. I stood in the convergence of motion beams. It was difficult to see anything other than the houses' dark outline in the glare. Some moments passed, I am not sure how many. I felt as though I was awaiting some total, blinding revelation. Then I heard a noise from one of the houses. It was a deep, anguished, bottomless cry, something you hear from your bed at night, coming from an unknown corner of the neighborhood, and maybe for a moment you think of investigating. Ultimately it's easier to let go, because it could be coming from anywhere, *could just as well be your own house*, so you keep to bed, glad you haven't interfered, although your sleep might be broken by echoes. I turned and hurried away, looking back over my shoulder until I reached the end of the block.

KYLE DIDN'T COME home that night. The next morning there was no sign of him in the orderly, lodger-like spareness of his room. I didn't make too much of it at first, figured the Lillys had overdone it on the family wholesomeness, OD'd on eggnog or something, though I did call the number on the creepy business card Cordelia Lilly had handed me, and then the F.C.O.D.P. itself, where I was greeted by a recorded voice asking for my credit card number. I gave up and drove to work.

Around eleven Boggs stopped by. He was wearing a new V-neck sweater and scarf, most likely of cashmere, although I didn't reach over to actually touch them. My employer was in a philosophical mood.

"So, Norberg, we've reached the end of the year," he observed. "Strange, isn't it, how the new year continues to hold the promise of renewal, no matter how many times we've seen a new year come and go, turning the calendar without changing ourselves in any significant way."

"True enough, sir."

"But we have good reason to leave this year behind, don't we? No question that something went awry for us. It must have been around the time your wife disappeared. I have to admit, there was always something a little . . . *implausible* about your marriage. I hope you don't mind me putting it that way."

Actually, I didn't like where this was going at all.

"The stunning and vastly talented wife. The insecure,

menially employed, vaguely creepy husband. And yet it was this unlikely fact that held everything in place, wasn't it."

"I'm not quite sure what you're getting at."

Boggs stroked the cashmere scarf as if it was a cat that had settled there. I wondered whether the scarf was a gift from his wife or one of his mistresses. "It was strange, Norberg, when your missus disappeared, when you became single," he said. "I felt myself growing diffuse. Seductions I might have achieved easily in the past became fraught and complicated. These were beautiful young paralegals and court reporters aware of my reputation. What's gotten into me? You've seen me destroying my archive. I had some remarkable letters in there, and some truly remarkable photographs."

I had heard rumors of the archive and fielded the occasional call from Jessica, Annabelle, or Bridget demanding the return of their materials. In my mind, the Boggs archive was as vast and criminal as a Bosch triptych.

"What's more, the cases aren't going our way," he continued. "I find myself dizzy in the courtroom, groping for a word just out of reach, and at times I completely forget about the defendant, and it seems that the judge, the jurors, and the prosecutor are gathered there in judgment of *me*."

"It sounds like you might want to see a doctor, sir."

"I don't know if there is a medical solution for this." He reached into the pocket of his peacoat and produced a small wrapped box. "A token of my appreciation for your efforts," he said. "In the new year, we'll have to assess where we really are and attempt to regain our footing."

He shook my hand awkwardly, then retreated through the front door. The gift was heavy in my palm and wrapped in blue paper with an intricate snowflake design. It was a magnifying glass.

THE GIFT CAME in handy when I finally got around to reading the morning's *Trumpet*, which offered a dense summary of the events that had taken place at the Central Library the day before.

The headline read ON HEROIC COP'S HUNCH, LIBRARY RAIDED; THIRTEEN ARRESTED. Underneath this was a large, soft-focus, hagiographic portrait of the Oracle. There was an aura of legend gathering around it already. The article recapped the librarians' seven-month standoff and city hall's increasingly harsh tactics as winter wore on. The Oracle had reportedly met privately with Mayor Fuller two days before Christmas, sharing his strong premonition that the library would soon be demolished, and the mayor, sick of the pause at the heart of downtown, had authorized a secret raid, circumventing his uncooperative police chief. At 6:00 A.M. on Christmas morning, the Oracle led a motley force of police officers, private security guards, and mayoral aides into the library. They quickly disarmed four shotgun-toting librarians who were changing shifts; from there, resistance was minimal, as the remaining holdouts emerged from their sleeping bags in the stacks. The dozen librarians, who had twenty advanced degrees among them, were arrested and charged with, of all things, disorderly conduct. Much was made of the fact that the raiders allowed them to bring library materials to read in jail, where they would be spending at least a few symbolic nights. That left only Cassandra Clark in her second-floor office. I thought of her burning memoirs up there under the portraits of fat three-piece-suited men with swollen knuckles and bronze watch fobs. Maybe she was thinking about men in power, how they would always be looming over her, whether in the form of these fading Victorian philanthropists or in the more loutish, illiterate form of Fuller. Maybe she was thinking that without Molly, none of it mattered. She did not respond to the barked commands of the officers. It was then that the Oracle, flanked by his partner, McCready, climbed the stairs to apprehend the "dangerous radical" and "experimental prose writer." According to the article, Cassandra Clark looked straight into the Oracle's racer shades and said: "You are overdue." The two ex-detectives dragged her out, earning florid praise from the *Trumpet* hack who was probably already rehearsing his award acceptance speech. The demolition of the Central Library was scheduled for mid-January, after a massive sale of library holdings to benefit the police officers' pension fund.

BY THE END of the day I'd heard nothing from Kyle, but I couldn't succumb to paranoia, I told myself. Instead of imagining the worst, I decided to go downtown and see Martin Breeze as I had promised. He seemed to have something important to say to me, and not something he wanted to communicate by phone either. I closed the office at six and hit the road in the hope of beating the traffic, but ended up in the thick of it, a slow creeping throng on the highway. Exiting I-99 early, I took the back way downtown through one of the city's grimmest neighborhoods, Fairgarden. It was a place of deep mythical danger. A number of post-apocalyptic films had been shot on location there. There were BEWARE OF DOG signs on the lawns and trash bags in the windows. The drug houses had transoms of art deco glass. Huge abandoned factories sunk back from the street like painfully shy old men whose glasses had fogged over. There was a graffiti artist who lived in an undisclosed basement around here. Something of a preservationist as well, because his specialty was tagging buildings that were about to be demolished by the city. There were some real gems in Fairgarden, late nineteenth century masterworks built with brass staircases, molded fireplaces, glazed brick. Their copper had been stripped and the windows removed from their casements. On the weatherizing boards the artist left his tag *BE* inside a large, convincingly 3-D wrecking ball that really seemed to swing. His art was an admonition to look closely at what was disappearing, in a neighborhood where no one wanted to look at anything closely.

They said you weren't supposed to idle at stoplights in Fairgarden, that it was best to push straight through, but I had no choice. An old black woman was crossing the street in front of me. A kid's blue winter coat was draped over her gaunt frame. She pushed a shopping cart full of white running shoes. They were massive, unlaced, factory-fresh. The broken traffic light bleated out a meaningless red as she pushed on, somehow, past the shells of buildings.

After abandoning Molly's car to the mercies of the night, I walked briskly toward the *Trumpet* building, frightened although I had nothing of value, my life included. Passing through the revolving doors, I was surprised at the amount of activity in the lobby. Reporters were enthusiastically supping in the adjoining greasy spoon, tossing bills on the table and hurrying off as they fastened nostalgic fedoras. It was far different from the glum hush I'd experienced on my previous visits to the building. They must have been energized by the library debacle, which had been picked up by national wires. For the moment, at least, until the story was wrung dry, they must have felt central in more than just geographical terms, capable of rekindling the *Trumpet*'s glory as they headed off for the prison, the tenth precinct station, the doomed library itself.

Still, I had to question the fact that, in these lean times, the *Trumpet* had hired an elevator operator. He held the metallic grate for me, overdoing it a little in his tight navy coat with rubbed brass buttons. Before I'd even finished giving him the number, he turned a lever, pressed a button, and we juddered up.

"Mr. Breeze mentioned that you two had an appointment," the operator said, revealing, at these close quarters, a new set of dentures and breath that smelled of sardines. "You should definitely find him up there, Mr. Norberg."

Unnerved by the operator's knowledge—which wasn't strictly a matter of doing his job well, I felt—I commented nervously that one didn't run into elevator operators much anymore.

"They say I'm very good at what I do," he said. "Very discreet." And with an awkward adjustment of the lever, which jerked the carriage to a halt, he disgorged me into what remained of the *Trumpet*'s culture department. The light in the hall was dim and faltering. I passed several desks that looked like they had been ransacked, proof copy littered everywhere, reference books splayed on the floor. Behind a milky glass door stenciled with the name L. P. BURROUGHS—LITERARY CRITIC was a vacant room in which a lone bulb hung over a spread-eagled inflatable woman, her red lips puckered. At the end of the hall, light wedged from Breeze's door; I moved toward it cautiously. It seemed best to knock, which I did, calling Breeze's name. A hum and a slight dripping noise was my only reply from the office.

I pushed the door open and found Breeze seated at his vintage Royal typewriter, which I'd assumed was solely decorative. He was sitting there very stiffly, completely upright as if he was posing for a mid-century secretarial manual. Breeze was not typing anything on the Royal, although there was a half-finished page stuck in the rollers. His fingers, which were poised inches above the home row, had a sickly bluish color—as I moved closer, I realized that the dripping sound was water rolling off his fingertips onto the keyboard.

His glasses, also, had second lenses of ice.

There was frost in his stubble and his thinning hair, lending a surreal dignity to his features. Purple bruises marred the right half of his face, and he leaned slightly away, as if weighted by the wounds. His stiffness was either the result of rigor mortis or the extended period of time he'd been left in some kind of meat cooler. Aside from the discoloration and the grimace, he was well-preserved.

The humming sound came from the space heater Breeze had told me about wanting the last time I'd been here—it was producing a stale warmth and had made some progress in melting Breeze's legs, judging from the pool of water that had formed around his ankles and spread on the carpet.

Even the scribes of the culture department would have struggled to evoke the sound my mouth made. All I could think to do was grab the page out of Breeze's typewriter, stuff it in my pocket, and look for a way down from the fourteenth floor that didn't involve a second ride with the so-called elevator attendant. I found a door for the stairs, but when I turned down the final flight, I was dismayed to see the attendant waiting there for me.

"Please allow me, sir," he said with a smile, holding the door. "When I'm given a job, I like to do it thoroughly," he explained.

I eased past him, hyperventilating into the putative safety of the lobby, and ran for the revolving doors.

"Watch your step, sir," he called after me, cheerfully.

Fairgarden was nothing after that. I chain-smoked on my walk back, finding the car untouched in its drift of soiled snow. I got in, locked the doors, and turned on the overhead light. There, against the steering wheel, I read Martin Breeze's final column.

THE ROCK SCENE

Fans of the Christian rocker Sebastian are devout in more way**s** than one. This brooding knight of faith has a small but intens**e** following of young people, many of them packed inside th**e** mall for his Christmas Eve concert. There was a screec**h**-ing roar when the lights went down, a full ninety minutes lat**e**. Wearing nothing but a long "hair shirt" and a white guita**r**, Sebastian held the crowd from the synth heavy opener "Celestia**l** Host" to the funky "Light is Eternal (Girl)." I must admit that **I** was distracted by his shrill voice and poor intonation. The lo**v**-ing fans disagreed, screaming. The high point of the performanc**e** came with the hit "Ballad of the Moneychangers," which even **I** will admit has a catchy hook. Ultimately, my first impressio**n** of this young singer was that he was entertaining up to a poin**t**, but that his combination of piety and lewd moves won't reac**h** serious listeners outside of the mallgoing teenage demimond**e** and their beleaguered chaperoning parents, at least for no**w**.

Tutored by Breeze's recent columns, I did not take long to find the acrostic he had encoded along the right edge the piece––though I was waylaid momentarily by the left-hand column's strangled and now poignant howl, "FtfmiWSH-wic-wobsa." *See her live in the w* . . . was Breeze's unfinished message to me. See her live in what? I thought about it, with Breeze's final prose work pressed to the wheel, insofar as I could think of anything except the critic defrosting in his office. A few minutes after I turned the engine to warm the car, it occurred to me. *Wozzeck*. Berg's *Wozzeck* was the opera's first production of the spring season; I had been sent a pair of complimentary tickets as always, my only Christmas gift. *See her live in*—well, it was called *Wozzeck*, not *The Wozzeck*, but I wouldn't be too hard on Breeze for his last gaffe. Though as usual this message was received with mixed feelings. An atonal opera about a German soldier losing his mind could hardly bode well. I shivered, checked my mirrors, and drove out of Fairgarden toward home.

MOLLY LIKED THE way people's voices sounded on our old answering machine. She liked the hum and whoosh of the old tapes that had been recorded and re-recorded a hundred times, the vinylish hiss, the voices barely afloat in static. When she was out, she had often serenaded the answering machine with parts of arias, which I would find on the tape when I got home. It had never occurred to me to save them. When I arrived home dazed from the *Trumpet*'s crime scene, I managed to process two facts. Kyle was still not there, and someone had called the answering machine, leaving a message long enough to fill almost the whole tape. What was on that tape was not going to be pleasant for me,

I could tell. I filled the tub with scalding water and poured a glass of wine. I thought of Martin Breeze and the powerful hand that had pushed down the lid of that freezer, then carried the frozen body back down the hall.

I hurried out to the kitchen, skirting the mirror, and brought back the answering machine. I set it on the back of the toilet, arranged my wine and cigarettes on the rim of the tub, and pressed play. Settling into the bath, I listened to the tape rewind. Something loosened in my body. I felt some sense of the relief Breeze might have felt when his brain turned off, relieving his muscles of their duties. For a moment, dissolving in the hot water, I almost felt like I had when Molly had touched my shoulders, all the pressure in my body going, as I let myself fall into the hands of the one person I didn't distrust.

The tape took a while to rewind. I half expected the voice on the tape to be hers, explaining it all. The tape clicked on, and there was only a hush at first, nothing but static and throat-clearing.

"Well, bucko, I guess you know who this is. This is Bob, this is Bob Lilly. We have your kid over here, he's fine, he's safe, I think he's asleep now. I just wanted to fill you in on that, bucko, because . . . well, I may be in the minority on this, but I don't think you're an evil man . . ." Here the tape became unintelligible, as Lilly exchanged words with his wife in the background. I knew what Lilly was going to say, that Kyle wasn't coming home, because Kyle didn't want to come home, and the Lillys now knew everything. Lilly continued on, beating around the bush, using words like "custodian," "malaise," and "unfortunate tryst," and I began to remember another time that I had suffered on account of this answering machine, which still had Molly's voice recorded on it. It was the only recording I had of her speaking voice, I realized. The only recording of her playing herself. *Hello, you've reached the Norbergs. If you have a message for Sven, Molly, or Kyle, please leave it at the tone.*

About two weeks before her disappearance, I'd found a message from Martin Breeze asking her to meet him at the Vantages Hotel. "I hope your husband doesn't get this," Breeze had said nervously, in the manner of someone aware that he is making an unfunny joke. Or maybe the joke was impossible to pull off with so much dead-serious desire going on beneath it; Breeze would have cuckolded me in a second, given the chance. He must have been thrilled to even pretend that he was arranging an assignation with Molly, rather than an interview for the *Trumpet,* in which my wife expressed her desire to "become someone else" when it appeared a week later.

I made a joke about it when Molly played the message in the kitchen. She was chopping an onion as Breeze's message played. "I bet Breeze reserved a room for the night, just in case," I said, and my own joke sounded just as forced as Breeze's had, curdled with fear. It didn't help that Molly took me literally.

"Martin Breeze?" she said. The knife fell to the cutting board beside her.

"I wasn't seriously . . ."

My wife's eyes were filled with tears, but whether genuine or onion-induced, I couldn't say. "You know, it is extremely tiring to live as a figure in someone else's paranoid dream. Extremely. Fucking. Tiring." She punctuated each of these words with a slash through the onion; her knife handle thudded the wooden cutting board.

I slid back deeper into the lukewarm water. My ears were

partly submerged, so I did not catch every word of Bob Lilly's monologue. I got the gist, though. It informed me that Kyle would be remaining with them as long as he felt this was the best option, and I should agree to this situation unless I wanted my "illicit relationship" to be made public. Meanwhile, I was still thinking of my wife at the cutting board, her eyes full of tears, and the message from Breeze, who was now defrosting a few miles away. I lowered myself further into the tub until only my mouth was not submerged.

Under the water it was like listening to some demented operatic trio.

Satanic actions, Bob Lilly sang. *Custodian, spiritual malaise, bucko.*

Paranoid dream, my wife trilled back. *Extremely tiring.*

I hope your husband doesn't get this, sang Breeze, leaking melted ice.

Then the tape clicked off and there was nothing but the drip of the faucet, heard from below.

18

THE HAVEN OF THE TRAUMHAUS WAS AHEAD. IN THE WEAK AND fumbling high beams, the trees looked stark; several scared animals fled into the depths, fleeing my predatory approach. I arrived strangely elated. The pines wavered in the wind. The rustle of pine needles and the rush of I-99 blended into a reassuring static. The lights in the patients' rooms, which brightened the squares of their windows softly but exactly, were half on and evenly distributed, giving the Traumhaus the appearance of a chess or checkerboard with no pieces on it. That is to say, no one was looking out. Those who were inside were inside. I showed my family member card to the desk clerk, who was absorbed in a weighty tome about some fellow named Zauberberg. He did not even look up at me.

The portrait of Bernhard on the landing depicted the architect at a long, unadorned steel desk, befitting his aesthetic. Bernhard leaned on one elbow, a pencil clamped between thumb and forefinger and aimed downward, jutting toward the climber of the stairs, almost threateningly. His ironic smile seemed to acknowledge this. As I climbed the stairs, I tried to meet the architect's eyes. It is surely pointless to stare down a figure in a painting, but in spite of this, or perhaps because of it, I let my gaze linger every time I arrived at the Traumhaus on the green and cloudy irises of the architect, framed by his thick black glasses. As I did so I realized that the painting had changed. Or, if I lived in a world where paintings did not change on their own, as I still believed I did, the painting had been altered. The alterations were minor yet significant. The two lenses of the architect's glasses had been darkened, concealing the two watery and suggestive pupils and the somewhat baggy folds of flesh that had cupped them. The vandal had done good work, using the same paint, the same slightly expressionistic brushstrokes. What should I have made of the fact that the architect's painted shades had the same tint as the Oracle's? I retreated down the stairs and stood before the doorway sentry's desk, clearing my throat several times before he looked up from his book.

"Yes?" he asked, annoyed.

"I think you've been vandalized," I said. "The portrait of Bernhard on the landing. Someone has . . ."

"Oh, I wouldn't know about that," said the sentry, only now sliding his bookmark in and closing his tome with a reluctant sigh. "I'm only the doorkeeper here. My job is to admit a select few and turn away the rest. That was what the classified ad said, verbatim. Everything else is beyond my purview."

"Well, that's fine, but surely," I said, "surely you've noticed the change in the portrait."

"The architect of this building was a very private man," the sentry replied, with the air of a government functionary reciting doctrine. "As you probably know, he spent the last months of his life here in almost total seclusion. Perhaps the sunglasses in the portrait represent this privacy."

"But," I sputtered. "As of last week he was not wearing sunglasses."

"I understand, Mr. Norberg," the sentry said, rudely reopening his book, "but I hope you'll understand that décor is not my area. I should add that it is unwise to become overly attached to any aspect of the Traumhaus. We do not deal in permanence here."

Under Bernhard's shaded gaze, I retraced my steps. Upstairs in the Wittgenstein Lounge, a formidable crowd had gathered around the TV. Backs to the placard that read THE LIMITS OF MY LANGUAGE ARE THE LIMITS OF MY WORLD, the distracted memoirists tuned in to the mayor's victory parade. The reception was choppy, almost avant-garde, due to the weather, but the residents didn't look shocked or dismayed by what they saw. Fuller, bald head agleam, rode in the first car of a motorcade down the newly christened Oracle Avenue. A row of shivering extras lined the curb, holding cell phones and Fuller re-election signs. As the motorcade passed, Fuller's limousine SUV to the Oracle/McCready cruiser, giant silk screen prints unfurled from the streetlights. The Oracle, cooler than ever in his triumph, regarded the street below from multiple postures of profound thought, his ever-present shades colored now tangerine orange, now magenta, now lime green. One after another they unrolled, vivid against the dirty snow, as Fuller's motorcade made its way toward the Central Library, already rigged with dynamite. "It's hard to remember anything . . . exhilarating . . . in Trude!" the newscaster exclaimed. The audience response was hard to gauge; a general melancholy pervaded the lounge and I sensed that their attentions were directed elsewhere. Onscreen, the revelers began a broken countdown to the Central Library's demolition. I turned away. The detonation sounded from the speakers as I went to look for my mother.

I WALKED DOWN the hall under the fluorescent tube lights. The lighting had been controversial with critics, as was the gray industrial concrete that arced high over my head. There was no comfort here, the critics had said, no assurance, the building did not embrace you but instead held you at a cold remove, and the lesser rooms were almost reminiscent of the anterior regions of those caves where our ancestors stored their dead. This was no way to treat the old and senile and chronically upset. But the mellow beauty of the pink and white fluorescents against the gray concrete won some of them over in time. It mirrored the moon on the snow outside, and maybe it made a counterargument of its own: that in the approach to death all familiar things become strange to us, as we lose their textures and the ability to hold them and even their names. The brutalist aspect of this hallway could be considered a kind of respect, an honest vision that was really no less troubling than the kitten posters, teddy bears, and religious kitsch that filled most homes of this kind.

The Traumhaus did provide a foot of shelf space outside each resident's door which displayed their relics, their trophies and tools and crafts, along with photographs of their younger selves and families. These shelves also held the inboxes where residents' memoirs were returned, on the first and fifteenth of each month, like paychecks. I was pleased to see that Mom's memoir had been stamped HIGHLY HARROWING. That meant she would be staying put in the Robert Walser Room, which she'd inherited from Vollstrom, who'd been demoted to the Kleist

Cabin. She enjoyed that room, and I enjoyed visiting her there, with its vista looking out on a staggered canopy of deciduous trees and the frozen pond trapping the wooden ducks, a wintry landscape Walser himself might have enjoyed walking through. He was a good patron for my mother, I felt: nervous, humble, uncertain. Maybe she would start writing her memoirs on napkins and the backs of postcards, as he had, in a script so tiny as to be almost invisible. A small library of his works was propped between two bookends on her desk.

I couldn't help lingering for a moment at the memory shelf. The photo of the three of us, Mom, Dad, myself, had been captured thirty years ago on an analog camera's Kodachrome. Maybe it was the result of the fluorescent light, but the colors in the photo seemed to have deepened over the years, and the ruddiness of our cheeks from the cold and the redness of my red coat, which I had no actual memory of, threatened to bleed into the snow. It was a dispatch from a world so far in the past it seemed fictional, those days before my father deserted us for a Swede named Claudia and the chairlifts of old Europe. His black-gloved hand was clapped on my shoulder and I stared into the camera with deerlike blankness. My nose was running. Mom was laughing beautifully at something, a joke my father had made, judging from the tremor of smile in his frost-encrusted beard, this moment of adult humor now lost to history.

Taking the bundled pages in, I flipped through my mother's manuscript. Having long since exhausted her childhood, adolescence, and the early years of her marriage, the only periods she remembered in any detail, her recent work had become spare and experimental by necessity, the thick forests of prose giving way to fragile saplings of text framed in white space. The lines she had punched into a mostly blank page resembled the snowy hill it described:

> *He flies over ice, his plumage tense and steely.*
> *The bright V hangs, and I sit with my son*
> *Waiting for him to come down.*
> *If he falls, will it be my fault?*

This brief verse had grown a tumor of commentary in three distinct hands: one of them, writing in red, had taken issue with the "steely plumage" image as a description of ski poles. A blue cursive hand critiqued the assonance of "falls" and "fault" in the last line, while the red hand disagreed. A green hand had circled the words "he flies" and "my son" and "falls" to no apparent end.

"This is very nice, Mom," I said, laying the manuscript on the edge of the desk. She turned from the manual typewriter where she was working. Despite widespread arthritis and eye problems in the Traumhaus, Bernhard insisted the residents type on manuals because they would be "redolent of bygone days." The physical difficulties of typing on them would "duplicate the awkward, painful process of recalling the past." An almost empty bottle of Wite-Out stood on the windowsill, sunk in a dried and caked moat of spilled fluid. There were a few spare ribbons and a date stamp that read TRUDE PUBLIC LIBRARY.

"I didn't hear you come in," she said. She tipped her reading glasses back into her thick gray hair. "What did they say? Have I gotten it all wrong again?" I shook my head and handed her the title page with its seal of approval. Her smiles wavered at the end like they'd forgotten their source. "They were right," she said. "I was sure that I forgot and mixed everything up and wrote it down wrong, but they were right."

This *they* concerned me at first, they could have been new phantoms in her house, but I soon saw what she meant. Even as she spoke the words she had one of Harris's little notecards in her hand. I recognized it right away. I could picture the silent comedian discreetly shedding it out of a suit sleeve or a false pocket. This was Harris's schtick, and the sentiments on this notecard my mother was now looking at—and similar ones strategically placed on every available surface in the room, I now noticed: the nightstand, the sill, the table, the mini-fridge, the closet door—weren't original in any way. They assured her that she was beautiful and smart and what she was doing was worth doing, and they were expressed in the most clichéd fashion imaginable. You could understand why he'd taken the vow of silence if this is what Harris had to say, and yet there it was: the proof of love, stashed in dozens of subtle places, where they would not stand out but would go on making their daily claims, telling my mother to believe in herself and hang in there, written with the full knowledge that they would be forgotten almost the moment they were read, only to be read again, believed for a moment again, forgotten again.

And to be honest I was overcome by Harris's simple little notes, his strategy to prevent losing the woman he loved, who was constantly receding from him. Would Molly have laughed to find one of these notes by her mirror? I left the room, closing the door behind me, and shook out in the fluorescent-lighted hall under the brutalist archway, knowing that however many times I told my mother that it wasn't her fault, I was the shade, unsteady and flickering, and it was the steady simple messages of the notecards that were necessary to her now.

* * *

VOLLSTROM ANSWERED THE door in a frayed and cigarette-burned pink bathrobe. He did not look well. His gray hair was greasy and had grown to his shoulders. He was shirtless under the robe and I could see his rib cage, the old cheesy skin stretched over it like cellophane. The Kleist was an oversized, windowless cubicle. The desk within was covered with stacks of paper, note-cards, legal pads, and Post-its, the detritus of a failed filing system. Near the top of the stack was the cover page of Vollstrom's December memoir, the verdict stamped plainly over his name.

He was not alone in the room. A young, scholarly-looking man with a pince-nez and blue medical scrubs sat in Vollstrom's reading chair, writing in a notebook.

"Norberg, may I introduce my new friend Frank, the orderly. We have been spending a *great deal of time* together lately."

Frank lifted his pen from the page and aimed it in my direction.

"Should I not be in here?" I asked.

"You may stay a while," Frank said. "The patient has not been having a productive day in any case, so it's just as well. However, you may not give him any cigarettes."

"Frank has been such a help to me here in the Kleist Cabin," Vollstrom said. "My god, the Kleist Cabin! What is next for me? The Franz Werfel? I've heard the most horrific things!"

Frank recorded this in his notebook.

"I see I'm digressing. Where was I? Ah yes, Frank. And his helpfulness. He prevents me from doing things that might actually aid my work, such as smoking, and instead distracts me with his shiny specs, the scratching of his pen, and constantly referring to me in the third person. Frank is just the amanuensis I need."

"That's enough," said Frank.

"There are rooms in the basement, you know," Vollstrom said to me. "You can hear the throb of the heater and the progress of bodily fluids through the pipes. They are named after writers so obscure that only scholars of the German language know how to pronounce them." He sighed, walked over to his bed, and fell back on the stiff mattress.

Judging from the action of his pen, the orderly devoted at least a paragraph to this movement.

"What can he possibly be writing?" Vollstrom asked. "How many ways are there to describe recumbency?" He seemed to register Frank's reproving look without even opening his eyes. "Yes, Frank, I know, there are innumerable ways, but the bread of experience grows stale. The same set of rooms, the same vistas. The demand for my work remains steady. Every two weeks, the next installment is required. It grows tiresome." He smiled wearily. His hair was arranged in an oddly symmetrical pattern around his head on the pillowcase, an ashen halo. "Suicide is much in my thoughts these days, of course, but in the end it would give Bernhard too much pleasure. No, I would not make it so easy for him. He'll have to go on trying to kill me with commentary, with the contradictory glosses, the tiny marginalia. Look at it, Norberg. The one who writes in red never agrees with the one who writes in blue. The one who writes in black is simply insane. Perhaps it is my friend Frank here, who I notice has a black pen in his hand."

Frank just shook his head and continued his note-taking.

I considered the demolished manuscript on the desk. The black writing was in all capital letters and in a smattering of different languages; the only thing clear about it was its hostility. The green writing consisted mostly of question marks and expletives. The commentary overlapped in several places, a whorl of words, and it was hard to disentangle even the more legible arguments of Red and Blue. I saw how it would be possible to think of all four sets of notes as extensions of the same mind, at war with its own moods. A kind of fugue.

"The Scheerbart Room, the Von Doderer Room," Vollstrom said. "Just try to think of the right word down there, and I promise the word will not be rehabilitation. When the work is going badly this does not seem like an assisted living facility at all, more like thwarted living, hindered living."

I assured Vollstrom that he was exaggerating. If Bernhard had really wanted him killed, I reasoned, he could easily have done so already.

"Yes," Vollstrom said, his words muffled by the olive blanket he'd drawn over his head, "but that would have been no *fun*. Just to have Frank snuff me with a pillow after dinner, which he would happily do. No, Bernhard is waiting and watching. He will kill me gradually as he killed the ducks. Death by criticism is slow and painful, the will is sapped, and when I no longer produce there will be no alternative. The notes of December do not bode well. Surely, that green handwriting is his."

I told Vollstrom that the green script didn't look like an architect's handwriting.

"They say some of his blueprints were illegible," Vollstrom said. "So this building may not be the one he exactly intended. It was unfinished at the time of his death, and certain errors and misreadings crept in. That's the only reason we can stand this place at all." He looked over at his bespectacled tormentor in the corner. "Are you getting this, Frank?" he asked. "The ideal building, for Bernhard, is always an empty one."

19

THE ORIGINAL OPERA HOUSE HAD BEEN BADLY DAMAGED IN a 1935 fire set by an anguished fan of then-reigning diva Olga Hillenbrund. The young Bernhard had presided over the 1941 renovation in a spirit of high camp. "The intention," as he explains in his *Memoirs*, "was to compile every possible excess of nineteenth-century ornamental architecture, for which I still felt some fondness at the time, and to rid myself of it all through sheer exaggeration." This would explain the two-ton chandelier, the gilt banisters, the enormous ceiling mural that depicted Orpheus's failed errand to the underworld. The public loved it, in a way they would never quite love another building of Bernhard's again. Young wags had their photographs taken on the grand staircase, next to the blinking gargoyles. The richly encrusted balconies had provided a backdrop for countless marriage proposals and unwise speeches of love. Far below Charon and his boatloads of Lethean dead, I toasted Jimenez. I'd found him lingering outside the ruins of the Central Library and, remembering his love for opera, offered him my extra ticket. He was wearing the clothes we'd bought for him at the Salvation Army thrift store down the street, baggy checkered pants and a crimson velvet smoking jacket. He didn't look any sillier than the surrounding bourgeoisie.

Having been denied backstage access, we waited for *Wozzeck*. Our pockets were stuffed with crossword puzzles and dessert tickets. Bubbles of talk slipped from mouths, blown nowhere in particular; the talk-bubbles, buoyant, rose to the ceiling where they popped, leaving no trace except a slight dampness in the air, which condensed on Madame Perloff's fur muff. The iron-ore baroness's headwear looked like a huge fur turban—if she hadn't owned a private box, it would have obstructed the spectators' view of her daughter. There was an ostrich feather jutting from it. When she leaned to tilt her ear toward the young man next to her, who was tapping notes into a phone, the muff slumped precipitously. A crowd of hangers-on condensed around the baroness. Caterers in German military uniforms tiptoed through the room, saying "*entschuldigungen Sie, bitte.*" A crowd of schoolchildren to our right, the baroness and her circle to our left, I began to experience a kind of *platzangst*, doubting that we could cut through the fizzy thickness of the lobby to our seats. The kids made a collective lunge for a large bin of cough drops, which they mistook for candy, while their teacher flailed his arms and bright scarf. This wave forced us to the fringes of the baroness's circle. She looked us over, intrigued, as if our proximity to her proved our inherent interest. Or maybe it was simply that her face, lifted and remolded so many times, assumed a permanent expression of high intrigue or alarm. She fixed us in her surgical gaze. Unsure if the baroness remembered our meetings of past years, I hesitated. The young man next to her stepped forward.

"I don't believe we've met," he said, with a British accent. "I'm Martin Breeze of the *Trude Trumpet.*"

I laughed in his face. "You're not Martin Breeze."

"Pardon me?" he asked. His phone began to vibrate and play the opening bars of *Eine kleine Nachtmusik.*

"He's not Martin Breeze," I said, turning to the baroness, "He must be some kind of . . . *impostor.*"

"An impostor!" exclaimed the baroness, grinning. She adjusted a ring of rubies on her white neck. "And what about you? Who are you?"

"A phantom of the opera," I replied. "And this is my friend the kidnapper," I said, putting my hand on Jimenez's shoulder.

"Oh, I see," said the baroness. "And do you collect ransom?" she asked flirtatiously.

The pseudo-Breeze was speaking into his phone. "There's some fellow here who disputes my existence," he said, smiling at me. "I think I must go and try to persuade him of my reality." He tucked the phone in the pocket of his beige suit.

"Martin Breeze is dead," I said coldly.

"I'm afraid I have to disagree with you there."

"Baroness, you must remember Martin Breeze," I said. "The critic."

As the pseudo-Breeze dug out his passport, the baroness said, "I do seem to remember a short, dumpy fellow who used to hang around here. His bow tie was never on straight. He did not look at home." Her pasted-open eyes lit up. "Maybe he should never have been here in the first place," she said. "Maybe he was the false Breeze, the impostor. I can assure you that *this* one can write decent prose."

And with that, no less a personage than Baron Perloff

stepped forward. The Baron wore a crimson tuxedo and a matching cummerbund over charcoal-colored slacks. He grabbed my shoulder with the proprietary intimacy that was the shared estate of drunks and the rich, and began murmuring hot, rank words into my ear. "I despise writers," he said. "They're like roaches. You kill one of them and a hundred more are born. Squirming to life with their tender souls already budding, the antennae poking through, already groping for unique insights and observations, it's filthy, the little red mouths, the teeth . . ." The baron shuddered. He jammed an imported cigarette into his silver holder. "The little teeth," he said.

The baron turned his shoulder, and I found our position in the circle had changed drastically. Throughout the baron's tirade, a squad of ushers in German surplus duds had been closing in on us, and they now had us surrounded, though for the moment they were keeping a polite distance, weighing deference against violence. "Are you gentlemen all right?" one of them asked, doffing a vintage infantry cap. It was the "elevator attendant" from the *Trumpet* building, I realized when he revealed his gleaming dentures. He was slowly rubbing an opaque, perfumed lotion on his knobbed and scarred hands.

"That man over there," I said, pointing to the pseudo-Breeze, "is not who he claims to be. He says he is Martin Breeze, who is dead, as you know."

"But you say yourself that Martin Breeze is right there." The elevator-operator-cum-usher smiled.

"I think we'll head to our seats now," Jimenez said, taking me by the arm. It was probably best to have an escort if you were descending into the underworld, which I seemed to be. We maneuvered through the school kids and reached the door, where another usher handed us a program. I regarded the deranged eyes and pale moony face of Wozzeck. I could not resist turning, despite Jimenez's protests. "Martin Breeze is dead!" I called loudly to the lobby, compelled to state the truth, even if it no longer could have any impact.

"No I'm not!" was the cheerful reply, then laughter, and the five-minute bell.

I COULD STARE for hours at Molly's face. She was my midnight double feature, my matinee. In my college dorm bed, I traced her topography: the ridges of her eyebrows, the sled-hill of her sharp nose, the pink ravine of her parted lips. At first she permitted, even enjoyed this point-blank spectatorship. "Why hello there," she would say, groggily waking. "You must be the night watchman." Insomniac that I was, I could at least rest my eyes on her. The motions of her chest were my fence-jumping sheep, and I tallied them to myself, sometimes picturing her ribs, lungs, heart, and blood working in concord beneath her skin. I would get thirsty or have to go to the bathroom, but I couldn't make myself leave the bed, unable to rip my gaze from her form. I didn't fully think through what it might feel like for Molly, to wake and find me staring hungrily at her, like I wanted to suck her in with my eyes. Some years later, in our house, she woke and said: "You know, that's kind of creepy. The way you watch me. I'm just sleeping here. It's not that interesting." I apologized and told her I wouldn't do it anymore. "It's no big deal, it's just a little weird," she replied, already losing consciousness again. I did my best not to stare at her as she slept. I stole a minute here, a minute there, turning if she stirred. The beige wallpaper on the other side of the bed was no comfort at all. It was like staring at a blank journal page, my own drab soul.

The operatic fan base was composed of similarly desperate, intent observers. Among the socialites and retirees, they filed in. Kyle's art teacher from Humboldt High, inspecting the paint chips underneath her fingernails. The nurse from my ophthalmologist's office. A cluster of laid-off librarians in vintage dresses and drugstore plus-ones. A shaky Frau Huber, leaning on her husband's arm. Brought here by rumor and innuendo, we waited for Molly to reappear, to guide us from the underworld carved out by her absence. In sharp contrast to the chatter in the lobby, a strange hush fell over the auditorium. Anything absolutely necessary to say was spoken in a whisper, as if speaking too loud might disrupt the air and spoil the atmosphere needed for her return. I was reduced to one among the many, her former husband. The lights darkened over us, creating a false night, and in the dark we felt ourselves pleasurably effaced, rubbed out: we turned our eyes to the stage. The heavy curtains parted to reveal a stark, minimal set. It resembled a still life in a high school art classroom. A child's papery yellow moon dominated the backdrop. Darkly expressive trees crept out from the corners of the set, casting weblike shadows in the pale circle of lighting. Stage left were two darkened figures, one man sitting in a barber's chair, the other standing over him, scraping a razor across his face. The razor's swipe was enhanced by sound effects, sending a serrated shudder through the audience. The orchestra sounded a dissonant chord, followed by a snare blow and some disconcerting little woodwind trills. The spotlight came up on the two figures: Wozzeck, in his uniform, played by the stocky tenor Andreas

Gutenberg, who had kissed my wife on several occasions. He shaved the figure in the chair, whose back was turned to the audience. The captain, or Hauptmann, was tall and had red hair slicked back over a pointed, oblong skull. The captain's back was turned to us, and his face was covered with shaving cream.

Langsam, he sang, *langsam*: "Steady, steady." My hands shook wildly.

I could not get a good look at Hauptmann in the chair. As I watched the scene, in which the captain berates Wozzeck about the bad manners of the poor (siring bastard children, pissing on walls), I tried to scrutinize the deeply familiar face. And yet Wozzeck's burly frame kept obstructing my view. It was almost as if the director had blocked the scene precisely to this end: Wozzeck kept spinning Hauptmann around in the barber's chair, dabbing a bit of shaving cream off his cheeks, ending up directly in my sightline. All I could see of the captain was one lathered cheek and his lumpy uniformed body, which looked heavily padded. His voice was an unusually high, almost chirping tenor—a voice in which I could almost, but not quite, hear some echo of my wife's. Staring at Hauptmann, I realized that I no longer remembered Molly's face as well as I thought I did—that years of research hadn't prevented her image from deteriorating in my mind. And yet, there was no denying that the tenor playing Hauptmann looked like Molly, or what Molly would have looked like had she been a man.

I flipped through the program. The cast notes included publicity shots of Andreas Gutenberg (as Wozzeck) and Ariel Perloff (as Marie), but when I got to the role of Hauptmann, played by Brian Molloy, there was only a gray square and the words PHOTO NOT AVAILABLE. The tenor's biography was masterfully vague: Molloy had been born in County Cork, Ireland, and supposedly studied at Trinity College in Dublin. He had performed in "major productions" of Strauss, Bizet, Mozart, and Verdi, and was delighted to "rejoin" the Lyric Opera for this show. When I looked up from my program, Hauptmann had been wheeled from the stage, and his place was taken by Ariel Perloff as Marie, who cantered out in a skimpy peasant smock. Perhaps her friends in high places had hoped that Ariel's deficiencies would be less obvious in an atonal opera such as this one, but they had underestimated the Trudian opera-going public. A group of grad students hissed when Ariel mistook an E for an E flat. They winced at her lax, sluggish phrasing and plugged their ears to her shrill attempts at the upper register. While the part of Marie would not have been out of Molly's range, it became clear that it was far beyond Ariel's abilities. Several of the grad students tied white handkerchiefs to their canes—a fad among composition PhDs—and waved them in surrender as Ariel attempted the lullaby in act two. The Baron and Baroness Perloff did their best to counter with bravos from their second-tier box, where they sat with the pseudo-Breeze and the thuggish usher, but they were outnumbered. A few seasoned buffs, librettos open in their laps, led the ironic, jeering applause when the child had finally been serenaded to sleep.

Hauptmann reemerged in act two alongside his insane compadre, the doctor, who sang a brief aria celebrating the theories that would make him immortal. I studied Hauptmann's awkward movements across the stage, the feigned quality of his sure, masculine stride. The egotistical doctor diagnosed Hauptmann. He hogged the stage, relegating Hauptmann to the background. There was a delicate, even feminine quality to the captain's voice and gestures, but before I could conclusively link them to Molly, the scene ended. At the end of the second act, the lights went up, waking me as if from a dream I had not yet understood and could not clearly remember.

At intermission, I walked upstairs to the balcony and joined the long line for the men's bathroom. The facilities at the Opera House were badly inadequate and a constant source of complaint. Male patrons of the Lyric Opera were forced to endure a subversive Bernhardian joke as they waited: the line for the bathroom snaked down the so-called Castrato Hall. A series of portraits and placards, celebrating the young singers who had sacrificed their manhoods for their art, hung over us as we inched forward, bladders smarting. There was a solemnity to our brigade.

I finally made it in, patronized the urinal, pulled the old-fashioned handle flush. On the way out, elbowing through the press of anxious faces in the narrow Castrato Hall, who should I come across but Herr Huber. He wore a blue wool suit that was threadbare at the knees and elbows. Huber avoided my eye and stroked his mustache nervously. I muscled through the line, ignoring protests, and grabbed his arm. The old music teacher was shaking. He attempted a few feigned pleasantries in his broken English.

"It's her out there," I said.

Herr Huber didn't respond; his trembling was noncommittal. I took his other arm and pinned him to the wall, under a large portrait of Farinelli.

"It's her, playing der Hauptmann," I said. "And your wife knew about it all along. Your wife trained my wife as a tenor. Transformed her. Helped her to disappear—from me. Tell me I'm wrong, Herr Huber."

There were murmurs of objection behind me, along with some weak attempts to disattach me from the aging Herr. The German stared at me with deep-set, bulging eyes, and I could see the strain his anatomy was under, the brisk pumping of an artery in his neck. He shrugged his shoulders and shook his head in desperate pantomime.

"You understand me perfectly well," I said. "Your wife helped my wife disappear. She helped her to change her voice. She arranged her new identity. Now Molly is Molloy, this man, this Hauptmann. Molly ist der Hauptmann. Tell me I'm wrong, Herr Huber."

"I don't understand," Herr Huber said.

"What I don't understand," I replied, "is why everybody keeps lying to me."

"*Was ist los?*" a deep voice inquired.

"*Seine Frau ist verschwunden,*" said another baritone voice. "*Und jetzt ist er verrückt.*"

"Let me go, please," Herr Huber said. Unconsciously I'd taken hold of his collar and tightened it around his neck. I knew that I would learn nothing more from Herr Huber, but at the same time, I couldn't let go. The frayed collar of his jacket was the closest I had come to the truth. I clung to it and stared at him furiously, until several capable hands grabbed me from behind.

"You've lost your act three privileges, buddy," the hand-rubbing usher said. He clamped my arms into his grip. "But don't worry, I'll tell you what happens." He lowered his voice and smiled. "He kills the bitch."

Two ushers carried me from Castrato Hall, down from the balcony on the grand staircase. The surplus army cloth rustled on either side of me. I didn't kick or struggle excessively as they manhandled me, recouping some sense of embarrassed civility now that it was too late. A crowd had gathered in the lower lobby. I knew many of these people, though it had been a year since I'd seen them. There was Andreas Gutenberg's wife and the assistant conductor, Gehrens. There was the stage manager and her husband, who'd had us over to dinner at their house a couple of times, years ago, and whose names had rubbed away. They looked at me with pity and a barely concealed delight, their necklaces and gold watches gleaming. I rode down on the guards' arms, between the gargoyles. There was Frau Huber standing by the dessert table. "Mathilde!" I cried, reaching for a first name that hadn't crossed my lips in years. "I know everything! I see it all now!" She held a large untouched slice of chocolate cake and wiped her eyes with her napkin. I could not look at them anymore, these sympathizers. I turned my eyes to the ceiling, which Bernhard had so beautifully restored. I counted the ferried dead as they took their journey of forgetting across the ceiling, until the ceiling turned to sky, and I was back out under the stars.

AFTER THE CLOSE of act three and the halfhearted applause, which I heard through the ducts, the lanky tenor appeared at the stage door. Molloy exited the property quietly, taking only one backward glance at the scene under the marquee, Ariel Perloff preening in an ambush of photo bulbs. He crossed the street, heading for the network of alleys that led through the old plazas. Molloy stuck his hands in the pockets of his coat—he walked with linear, masculine impatience, with no trace of Molly's pendulant, fluid walk. Had he been practicing this, I wondered?

Molloy kept pace with his shadow, projected along the back walls of old brick warehouses. The shadow seemed to lead him along; he was leashed to it. We passed a boarded cinema that had once shown foreign films, and then had a second life showing foreign softcore films, and finally a third life showing hardcore films, before it went out of business. The boards made it look ashamed, overcome by a final, improbable modesty.

When Molloy reached the plaza, he stopped suddenly and looked both ways before turning back to face me. A yellow streetlight outlined his lanky body and projected an even thinner duplicate across the cobblestones. I tried to hide against a brick wall imprinted with the slogan PERLOFF IRON ORE IS OK, but Molloy had seen me.

"Simon?" Molloy said, his voice sounding hoarse, desolate, small.

"Molly?" I replied, stepping forward.

The thin tenor stepped forward to scrutinize me. As he approached, I was confronted by a set of deep blue eyes, an unfamiliar jawline, a superfluous mole. I was forced to admit, here at close range, that my myopia had helped to forge a Molly out of the redheaded blur playing Hauptmann in the Opera House.

"*You're* Simon?" the tenor repeated, looking hugely disappointed.

"It's Sven," I said.

He looked me over again and shrugged. "I was meeting a blind date."

"He could still show up," I said. "Maybe he's just late."

"I sincerely doubt it," Molloy said, kicking a stone across the square. His lifted foot was shod in an adolescent's canvas sneaker. The momentum of the kick spun him around, and he spiraled closer to me, looking me up and down again as he did so. "I know you from somewhere," he said.

"Remember Molly Norberg?" I asked.

"Good God," he said. "You're the husband. Of course." Molloy took a few steps away, veered around a dried-up fountain.

"I thought she was you," I said. "I thought she had become you."

"You must have had pretty bad seats," Molloy replied.

"Yeah, and I forgot my opera glasses."

"You didn't miss much—tonight anyway," Molloy said. He scanned the square a final time for his absentee blind date. "Well," said Molloy, "he isn't coming. I should sing a fucking aria about it. Walk me partway home, will you?"

He led me down another short alley back to Oracle Avenue. The traffic was thinning out as opera patrons made their exits from downtown onto I-99. Overhead, the Oracle's grinning image wavered in tangerine, teal, chartreuse.

We walked toward the river. Everything had closed up, in this part of town, except for a check cashing outlet and some so-called chop suey stands. A couple of urban decay tourists clacked past in a horse-drawn carriage, shaking their heads. We stopped in front of a closed-down department store. It had had an earlier incarnation as one of three Wagnerian appreciation cults that had thrived in fin de siècle Trude. In another life, I could have been the secretary here. The urgent banners of a clearance sale still dangled from the rafters. The lights were on. Mannequins held the window display, a proud line of blank torsos and whisk heads.

Molloy slumped down under an EVERYTHING MUST GO sign. "I could use a cigarette," he said.

"Isn't it bad for your voice?" I asked, handing him one.

He shrugged. "Gives it some edge, some texture."

We sat quietly for a moment in the store's bargain afterglow.

"Did you know Molly well?" I asked.

"No, not at all," Molloy replied. "Although she did fill in for me once, last season. You must have heard about it. I was singing the part of Don Ottavio in *Don Giovanni*. My partner at the time . . . well, he was also the understudy, and we kind of gave each other this cold." He smiled. "So she had the chance to display her marvelous range." Molloy pulled on his cigarette, the tobacco crackling. "And everyone, of course, was thrilled with it, with her. Molly, Molloy, what's the difference, they said. She had a way of leeching the spotlight, your wife. But very gracefully. Most people didn't mind in the end."

Molloy finished his cigarette and began walking toward the river again. His stride was long. I had to jog a little to catch up to him. "The kind of talent she had, it was sort of superhuman," he said. "It made people like Ariel Perloff look . . . well, your wife's voice exposed them. It exposed mediocrity." In the distance a siren sounded, and Molloy's attention seemed to drift in its direction for a moment. He paused to consider his words carefully before going on. "The Perloffs, I mean the baron and baroness, really didn't care for your wife," he said. "Here's an accomplished mezzo, late thirties, still in her prime, never misses a show. A genuine coloratura mezzo who can sing roles on either side of her true range. It really looked like Ariel was going to be an understudy for life. And rightly so. I mean, you heard her tonight. Part of me wanted to go over there and push her off-stage myself."

"Do you think they did it?" I asked.

"The Perloffs?" asked Molloy. "Well, I don't know. *Did it*, that's a bit strong. Not that they aren't capable of such crude jobs. They pay off a few cops, send out one of their 'employees.' A name like theirs goes a long way in this town. But Molly? No, their approach to her had to be somewhat different. She was, certainly, under a great deal of pressure right before she disappeared."

We fell silent as we reached the old granaries along the Gertrude River. The abandoned mansions of industrialists hung over the water, some simply boarded up, others half-destroyed by fire, their charred frames resembling the ink-stained fingers of clutching hands. It was impossible now to recapture the hope these whiskered men must have felt, gazing down at the river from their windows at night. As it turned out, the river itself had proved to be their undoing—its tendency to dwindle during drought years, blocking the arteries of commerce. At these times, the Gertrude was a mere stream, and the struts of the Gertrude Bridge looked like the obscenely exposed legs of a skinny girl wearing ankle socks. The Gertrude Bridge was the official suicide bridge of Trude. It had been named after Gertrude Grunewald, née Trudenhauser, the mayor's daughter, who had been the first to avail herself of this bridge. She had jumped to escape her husband, a salt magnate who turned brutal after his mine collapsed in 1897. Mayor Trudenhauser, who had advocated the marriage, was overcome with remorse, and from the depths of his grief he pushed through a strange piece of legislation that has made Trude a suicide destination to this day. The law, passed by a glum city council in the post-Exhibition days of 1899, stated that any citizen choosing to end his or her life on the Gertrude Bridge would be memorialized by a small bronze plaque. "It may be some consolation to these desperate souls," Trudenhauser famously remarked, "to know that our city will remember them." Many lawmakers have attempted to reverse the statute over the years; however, they have never succeeded, on account of Trude's large and surprisingly well-organized Gertrude Bridge Group—the most diverse and effective suicide lobby in the Midwest.

As Molloy and I approached the bridge, over a century after Gertrude's death, the names covered both sides, the undersides of the arches, even the sidewalks themselves. The gauche, unillustrious names of my fellow Midwesterners, the Hanks and Trishes, the Patties, the Dougs. With the river as high as it was that night, some of the plaques were submerged, as if they too had jumped, unable to bear the light of the moon. Those above the waterline were reflected in a wobbling scrawl on the river. The Gertrude carried broken branches, pop cans, and dead fish. Beneath the surface, sluggish carp twisted through her soft and murky depths. It was no fait accompli to jump from the Gertrude Bridge—for every finished name on the bridge, there were two who'd failed, who'd leapt at the wrong angle or at the wrong time of day, when the Trude police trawler was on the water. How horrifying to be sucked back out of that cushioning sediment among the carp and the pop cans and cigarette butts like the one I now dropped to flutter and hiss out, pulled back to life.

"I think I'm losing my mind," I muttered.

"Pardon?"

"You sang very well tonight," I said.

"Thank you," Molloy said. He smiled. "That's sweet of you."

The red-light district, with its strip clubs, all-night bars, and massage parlors, was across the Gertrude. Molloy was heading toward those lights, which bleated from far away. He extended his slender, manicured hand. "Thank you for being my blind date," he said. "And I'm terribly sorry for your . . ." He fumbled for the right word. "I really am sorry." He glided off over the plaques of the dead, fading into the distance—he became a smudge, a smear, blending at last into the roseate glow of the west bank. With nowhere to go, no one to look for, I stumbled around reading them. Irrationally I began to scour the bridge for Molly's name, as if she might have jumped here without me or anyone else knowing. But I found no Mollys. Her name echoed through my mind like a foghorn, plangent and hollow. Molloy was completely gone now. There was no one else on the bridge. There was no one inhabiting the merchants' mansions. I was ideally placed, I thought. I stared down into the muddy depths of the Gertrude, where so many of my fellow townspeople had taken their rest. I imagined the sediment's soft embrace, wedging the toe of my dress shoe into the stone railing. Only the thought of my name on a plaque dissuaded me in the end.

20

SOME WEEKS LATER I RECEIVED A MESSAGE FROM BOB LILLY stating that my son had been accepted into college on early admission and wanted to see me to share the good news. This was a lie—the part about him wanting to see me, anyway—but that didn't surprise me, coming from Bob Lilly, who withheld the name and location of the notorious "college." We'd agreed to meet at the Traumhaus so that Kyle could see his grandmother at the same time, but when Lilly failed to appear at the agreed-upon 5:30, Mom started fretting about her place at the dinner table and I figured it was just as well to let her go. I led her up the hill from the pond where we'd been feeding the new ducks, who looked for all purposes like a perfect family, though I worried for the ducklings in their obedient line. The Traumhaus dining room was on a cantilevered porch, a floating mirage of candlelit fellowship on the hillside. The early arrivals were already taking their places at long lacquered tables. I sent Mom upstairs, watched her fade into that patterned brightness. She wouldn't have had much to say to him anyway, with only a few rags of language to her name.

I returned to the parking lot to wait. Lilly's van was indistinguishable at first from the other shadows encroaching on the Traumhaus garden. A slight wind began to blow the birches and the oaks, whose last tenacious leaves were falling to the gray earth. After some whispered counsel from Lilly, my son disembarked from the kidnapper van. Kyle had grown at least a foot, it seemed. He wore a corduroy blazer with wide pointed lapels that might have belonged to Lilly. A straight black tie dangled from his collar. Striding forward with the swagger of a car salesman, he reached for my hand.

"Dad," he said, crushing me in his grip.

"Son."

Lilly must have gotten him something helpful for his face. The roughness and pox I remembered, and had come to love, had given way to an innocuous zit or two and some minor shaving damage.

"You look great, kid," I said, resisting the urge to trace the old psoriasis scars with my finger. He didn't return the compliment, not that he honestly could have. I knew how I looked. We walked up to the Traumhaus lobby, passed under the doubtful eye of the sentry, and continued through the back door. There were a few other visitors and residents strolling through the sculpture park. This inner courtyard of the Traumhaus was superbly groomed. Maintenance guys in gray shirts were out salting the paths. It was an astringent Midwestern March evening, the kind of night that gathers power from the vast blanknesses of the plains. Flurries wheeled through the garden, pushed by a slight breeze. We walked the tended pathways.

The sculpture park had been constructed in the spring, summer, and autumn of 1983. By then Bernhard had already moved into the Schreber Suite to begin his last decline. Creative struggles over the park, for which he had commissioned twenty-nine site-specific pieces, consumed his final summer and accelerated his illness. A series of photographs in the front lobby showed the architect donning V-neck sweaters and collar-heavy polyester shirts, in postures of tense détente with the sculptors on his payroll. It was all supposed to resemble *ein andere Welt*, another world. I walked alongside my son, past the same massive sculptures that had dwarfed the architect in photographs. Big steel slabs jutted out of the earth, painted the pinks and aquamarines of early 1980s avant-garde. Nearby, a circle of rusted ballistics evoked a prayer circle of some defunct and giant race. Kyle glanced sideways at the sculptures as he passed. He wanted to get through the space, through the conversation. A ten-foot marble eyeball observed us through its cloudy pupil.

"Do you still have your marbles?" I asked.

He laughed, rolling his eyes up toward the clouded sky. I noted the transformation in my son, from the easygoing, confident adult he'd resembled minutes ago to the sullen teen he became by default in my presence. He slouched his shoulders to indicate his dismay at being with me, crumpling himself up inside the corduroy blazer. As we walked, and I tried to think of what to say, I became aware of a flickering presence behind us. It was no more than a thought at first, a servant of the encroaching dusk. Something disturbed the edge of my vision.

"So I suppose Bob told you," Kyle said.

"Told me what?" I asked.

"About bible college."

"Yeah," I said. "He did."

We followed a suggestion in the grass—not so much a formal path as a rubbed consensus—around two pools of half-frozen water that encased a few balled leaves. Evening had crept over the garden, weaning the sculptures to their silhouettes. A bare slope led down to the cracked and netless tennis courts. On the edge of the hill stood a large work in bronze and graphite; the sculptor had titled it *Adolescence*. It was a giant hand jutting from the hill in a gesture of salutation or affront. The thick wrist looked rooted in the hillside. Kyle stepped closer, gazed at the daunting fingers, the gnarled trunk-like wrist. In the shadow of the powerful hand, Kyle supplied me with details of the college, its supposedly rich tradition of evangelical and charity work. It was two hundred miles away in a cornfield. I pictured a row of old brick dormitories, an avenue of oaks. To visit him there, I would have to drive long hours down interstates bordered by neon crosses on one side, neon adult video stores on the other, roads otherwise dark and devoid of comfort.

"Bob Lilly," I asked, "is an alumnus?"

"Yeah." Kyle considered the vacant tennis courts. "He wrote me a recommendation."

On closer inspection, the sculpted hand was a detailed, even meticulous work of realism. Its nails were dirty, it had unruly bronze cuticles and a horizontal cut along the knuckle of its ring finger.

"I didn't expect you to approve or anything," Kyle said.

"I do approve, I do approve," I said. "I couldn't be happier. Now do you still want to go?"

He scoffed. "Bob didn't even want me to come here," he said under his breath, but the garden was so still, I had no trouble hearing him. "I thought it would be the adult thing to do."

"What do you know about adulthood?" I asked. I leaned

over, managed to get a smoke lit sheltered by the hand, then stayed choking on it for a moment. "Seriously, you don't know shit, and you should be glad. It's a long, slow process of losing everything that matters to you."

His reply was spoken in a harsh, throaty rasp. "That's what happens when you worship a human being, Dad." He shook his head fiercely and took two hard breaths. He retreated behind the hand, tracing his fingers along the metal, and as he disappeared I had an inopportune memory of a hide-and-seek game we'd played years before. When he spoke again his voice was disembodied, it was as if the hand was speaking to me.

"It shouldn't have surprised you," Kyle said, through the hand. "You were there. You heard her, just like I did."

"Heard what?" In fact I did hear something, a rustling movement in the shrubbery behind us. At the distant Traumhaus, the first lights were coming on: a cone of lamp in the Robert Walser Room, TV in the Wittgenstein Lounge. Pale lights, muted and austere.

"You heard her crying," Kyle said. "You heard Mom crying, every night."

His eyes blazed from the dark as he emerged. Now that he was out in the open, facing me, I looked away, staring up at the fourth floor of the Traumhaus, the bright windows of the exalted Schreber Suite. I wondered how the occupant of that suite would describe the indistinct and distant world below, from such a solitude and such a height. The starved world of scrawled trees and tiny dot-like beings could resolve itself into a single letter, *S*, which signified pain, or simply feeling, or the first letter of a name. *S* could not help me now. I knew as well as Kyle that tonight was the kind of night that made Molly cry. *I used to search for my wife*, I thought. *I used to search for my wife every night downtown.*

"I'll pray for you, Dad," Kyle said, walking into the Traumhaus's shrouded glow. In the parking lot, the gray van coughed to life, its headlights flashed on, and it pulled to the curb for him. There was no question of intervening this time. The best and most dignified thing I could do was nothing. Lilly got out of the van and I watched their two forms converge for a hug in the dusk. Kyle's kind and charitable guardian turned to give me one last look, in which his kindness and charity were suppressed. An utterly neutral stare directed both at me and the bronze hand behind me, without any distinction of these two objects in his visual field. I watched the two passengers climb into the van and turn toward the I-99 frontage road. It was the last time I saw Kyle for several years. The next time I saw him was on television, preaching; by that time, of course, he had changed his name to Lilly.

AFTER HIS DEPARTURE the sculpture garden was silent. I sat down under the hand, which was, I thought, useless, unpartnered, incapable of prayer. I sat numbly in its shadow for a period of time, until the malingerer I'd sensed all along emerged at last. He wore his frayed pink bathrobe, grubby opaque slippers, and the remains of a sweater.

"I smell cigarettes," he said.

I handed him one and asked how he'd managed to get away.

"My memoir put the orderly to sleep, again." Vollstrom grinned. "Of course, that's the paradox of our memoir-writing regimen here: there's nothing to write about."

"You're going to catch pneumonia," I said.

"Hopefully!" Vollstrom exclaimed, lighting his cigarette

with a damp match. "Pneumonia has always struck me as a lovely flower of disease."

"I think my wife left me," I said. I could hardly say what compelled me to speak or where the words had come from. They exited my mouth softly, leaving no imprint except for the evanescent steam of my breath. The moment I spoke these words I wanted to grab them back, bury them deep in the earth where no one would find them. How could I recover from this admission? *It was me, the gray man*—I was dizzy, my chest throbbed as if I'd been beaten. I squeezed my eyes shut and through the burning saltiness saw the image of Molly in the sunlight, laughing and smiling at me. She extended her hand to my cheek.

I felt a leathery hand on my shoulder. It was Vollstrom's. "Congratulations!" he said, flashing his yellow teeth. "Now you will almost certainly be admitted here, and you already have a subject for your memoir. Few can say as much. With some luck and competent judging, I'd expect you to make the Klaus Mann Chamber within a year or two. You could even be a potential candidate for the Schreber, the Schreber is by no means beyond the realm of possibility."

"That is not my ambition," I said. "I want to get out of this place."

"Leave Trude!" Vollstrom had a good laugh at this. His laugh turned to a cough and he spat a sallow chunk of lung into the snow, his white legs shaking. "But that's impossible," he said.

"It was possible for my wife. She got out somehow."

"Well of course! For some it's possible. But for certain souls, souls like yours or mine . . . or Bernhard's. Look at Bernhard, the exile's exile. Look around you at the high moderne castle he built for himself. Clearly such an individual could never leave Trude, despite the vitriol he spouted against it in his later years. Yes indeed, despite everything he said, Bernhard was what you call a *homebody*." Vollstrom began to laugh again and asked me for another cigarette. "You're sitting on his grave, by the way."

To Vollstrom's great amusement I moved some snow with my feet and revealed a small recessed stone. Its inscription was barely legible in the faint light:

KLAUS BERNHARD (1909–1983)

HE ATTEMPTED TO CREATE A WORLD HE COULD LIVE IN

"Don't worry, he loved the idea that people would be walk-ing all over his grave, sitting on his grave," Vollstrom said. "I don't think you realize what a funny guy he was."

Then Vollstrom, who was one of the last original inductees to the Traumhaus, began to tell me the story of the architect's last days. I will record it as accurately as I can on the stiff keys of this manual typewriter, from these heights of estrangement. The pond and the ducklings are far below. These days I can hardly remember how it felt to have a wife and son—to be a family man, as they say. There is no question that Vollstrom's story was highly dubious, but he was there to witness Bernhard's death first hand, and the probable inaccuracy of his account does not mean that it is without value, exactly. He spoke slowly between drags on his cigarette, which he neglected for long stretches. It shed small wads of ash onto Bernhard's grave.

By the winter of 1983 the architect was in terrible health, Vollstrom began amid the falling flurries. The winter of 1983 was one of the coldest on record. The roads to the Traumhaus were blocked, and the orderlies had to go out in snowshoes to retrieve the necessary supplies. In the Schreber Suite Bernhard lay dying. Years of prescription drug abuse had left him yellow and nephritic. He was exuding an unbearable stench, the stench of someone who is rotting from within. There was a brutal irony in this, Vollstrom noted, which Bernhard himself might have appreciated in a better mood. The architect who had been reluctant to install bathrooms in his buildings, where visitors might expel their wastes, was now being killed by his own, which were trapped inside him and poisoning him, creating such a horrible odor that no one could stand to be near him for very long. The architect was entirely alone in the Schreber Suite. He was feverish and hallucinating. From his isolated penthouse, Bernhard ranted incessantly. He cried that he was freezing solid, that his right hand had broken off and had fallen in his lap. My blood is hardening, turning to ice, the architect cried, according to Vollstrom. He began a long diatribe against the city of Trude. This city will never amount to anything, he cried from his stinking chair. It is only right that most people see this city from the air—as a distant grid it is much more beautiful and appealing, whereas on the ground it is full of mediocrities who long to see their paralysis reflected and magnified in the city around them. Trude teems with such mediocre people, they cannot imagine in their wildest dreams a better life, they are enthralled by their own aura of failure, they would actually feel uncomfortable if their city became a desirable place to live. They want to prevent any kind of excitement, any artistic accomplishments beyond the familiar, they are terribly afraid of foreigners, their nepotism is nauseating. They cast aspersion on anyone who might enhance their quality of life, who might enrich the city where they live and make it desirable, when they see a work of

211

beauty they are immediately suspicious and hostile, they hate the person who has challenged the morass in which they so comfortably reside, these middlers in the middle . . . *das Mittel* . . . *mein mall!* My mall! Look what they did to my mall! It's killing me! Bernhard lapsed in and out of his native language as he spoke to no one in particular from the Schreber Suite. To the patients who were forced to listen through their walls, understanding nothing, Bernhard's rant was at times reminiscent of atonal song. *Ich sterrr-bbe*, he half-sang. I'm dyyy-ing, he cried in his surprisingly rich baritone, which resounded through the asylum. One might even credit the rants of the dying architect with a strange beauty, Vollstrom said in one of his more charitable moments, tapping ash on the grave.

As the snowstorm continued, the architect's condition deteriorated—if it is possible to speak of deterioration at this point, Vollstrom said with a laugh. Bernhard's monologues turned from his hatred of Trude to his early life in the Austrian Alps and the village he had been forced to leave by "the Mustache," as he now called Hitler. In Bernhard's final hours, he shouted about snowmen. His lifelong fascination with snowmen is well-known. A famous passage from his *Memoirs* recounts the moment when Bernhard and a friend stood admiring the figure they had just crafted from fresh Alpine snow. The friend ran off to join a snowball fight down the street, but Bernhard was unsatisfied. He stared at the snowman. "Where is his house?" Bernhard asked to no one. A moment later he began constructing that house from ice and packed snow. The snowman, for Bernhard, was inextricably bound up with architecture itself, with his entire life's work. Now that he was at death's door, as they say, Bernhard spoke of nothing but snowmen. His circular rant zeroed in on a single point, which he repeated endlessly. *Sie müssen Schneemänner bauen*, said the sallow architect who was pickling in his own urine. They must build snowmen, they must build snowmen, they must build snowmen, he repeated with an urgency that left no doubt this was his final request, said Vollstrom. Again he began to sort of sing the words in his deep baritone voice. The orderlies ignored him at first, as they had disregarded claims of detaching body parts and his various abuses of Trude. They had become so used to tuning out the voice with the German accent that it took a real effort for them to understand his words. When they could no longer tolerate the loud singing, *sie müssen Schneemänner bauuen*, the orderlies consulted among themselves. The request was highly irregular and certainly dangerous. But despite his horrible smell and incoherence, despite his profanity-laced attacks on each of them in the past days, there was still a certain reverence for Bernhard at the Traumhaus. Indeed there still is, Vollstrom said, tapping ash on the grave. The orderlies informed the most able patients that they would need to get their coats, hats, and mittens on, because they were going out to the grounds. Vollstrom was one of these patients. By this time, it was dark.

An unlucky staffer, holding his breath, went into the Schreber Suite and wheeled the dying architect to the window. The reeking and irascible German kept shouting. My nose is freezing, my ears are freezing, my toes and fingers are freezing, now my ankles are freezing, my knee feels frozen, the architect cried, as if he were a child trying to fall asleep. Mummified in his foul blanket, he had a direct view of the bewildered patients who stumbled out in the snow. Vollstrom described the extreme disorientation of the motion lights that tripped and flashed, the thick and swirling snow, the putrid Bernhard hunched like a shrunken grandmother at the window. Many of the Traumhaus patients did not remember how to build a snowman. They became confused, drawing stick figures in the snow with their canes or falling backward to make snow angels. Vollstrom and the other veterans showed the rest what to do. They all began building snowmen for Bernhard's benefit. Their efforts were strange and disfigured. Some collapsed, others did not resemble human beings at all.

"I sometimes think that I am insane myself," Bernhard writes on the last page of his memoir, "but perhaps if I were sane I would never have built anything." The spectacle on the hill seemed to calm him, said Vollstrom. As the fumbling, uncertain patients worked on their snowmen, and Bernhard watched them from the best seat in the house, he suddenly began to laugh. The laugh started low in his chest and rose from there, perhaps the way a spirit might leave a body, with a certain buoyancy. According to Vollstrom, the architect's laughter had a chilling quality as it carried on the wind over the snowy grounds outside, where Traumhaus patients were now slipping and falling on the hill. They buried their faces in their mittens and batted at their abortive snowmen. The situation had become unbearable, said Vollstrom, the cold and the snow and the architect's laughter. It was at this moment that Bernhard spoke his last words. "It is my own Ulli who is buried under that labyrinth," he cried, and according to Vollstrom, his laughter turned to a howl of despair as he said this, though others at the scene disagreed. "My own Ulli is buried there, under the labyrinth," he repeated, and having disburdened himself of this information, he slumped to the side, his wasted body covered with snowflakes. Out on the hill, the patients stood silently for a moment, next to their half-built

snowmen. They observed a moment of silence for their dead architect. It was an extended moment of silence—they had not had quiet for days. At last the orderlies called everyone in and the motion lights snapped off.

There was an excavation of sorts done at Bernhard's shopping mall a few weeks after his death, said Vollstrom. The authorities poked around under the labyrinth for a while to see if there was any truth to Bernhard's last words. A thorough excavation of the labyrinth would have taken months, however, and would have cost the current owners of the mall many thousands of tourist dollars. The superficial search was inconclusive, leaving Vollstrom to wonder if Bernhard really had "revealed the secret of the labyrinth" after all, or if the dying man simply had one last joke in him before he died, on the coldest day of the coldest winter on record. Who knows what that laughter meant, if one can even speak of meaning, Vollstrom said. He held out the possibility that the laughter was only a cover, that Bernhard was, in fact, being as painfully, nakedly earnest as he had ever been in his life. After all, Vollstrom said with a slow smile, when the same excavators went to Ulli von Hartsig's grave, where the profit motive did not prevent them from making a thorough search, they found her half of the tomb empty.

ACKNOWLEDGMENTS

TEDDY WAYNE HAS BEEN A TIRELESS ADVOCATE AND A TRUE friend. This book would not exist without him.

I am grateful to my mentors all along the way: Myrna Klobuchar, Annie Dawid, James Wilcox, and particularly Kathryn Davis, who helped me raise the scaffolding of this book.

For their insightful early readings of the manuscript, thanks to Jessica Baran, Stefan Block, Sarah Bruni, Deborah Eisenberg, Beth Parada, and Kellie Wells.

Liese Mayer, editor extraordinaire, found all the things I missed—her grace and discernment imbue these pages. To Peter Mayer, Michael Goldsmith, Mark Krotov, and everyone else at the Overlook Press, thanks for believing in my work and presenting it with such style. Thank you to my agent, Renee Zuckerbrot, and to my first friend in the business, Rosalie Siegel.

To my parents, Arlene and Paul, and my brother, Mark, for your patience and love.

Eleanor, you know who you are.